T0350019

OLD WORLD

THE FRENCH LIST

Fabienne Kanor

OLD WORLD

TRANSLATED BY
LYNN E. PALERMO

LONDON NEW YORK CALCUTTA

PAP
TAGORE

The Work is published with the support of the
Publication Assistance Programmes of the Institut français

Seagull Books, 2025

First published in French as *Louisiane*
by Fabienne Kanor
© Editions Payot & Rivages, Paris, 2020

First published in English translation by Seagull Books, 2025
English translation © Lynn E. Palermo, 2025

ISBN   978 1 8030 9 393 2

British Library Cataloguing-in-Publication Data
A catalogue record for this book is available from the British Library.

Typeset by Seagull Books, Calcutta, India
Printed and bound in the USA by Integrated Books International

To David

Le Malheur de l'homme est d'avoir été enfant.

Frantz Fanon
Peau noire, masques blancs

my arms broke, they broke my arms with rocks, my spine is twisted, they wrenched it, and in the end, I buckled, I dropped to my knees, I don't have enough feet to run anymore, one day, they gave my tongue to the dogs and I opened my eyes to look at the road, a long time ago, when I walked on the earth and I was beauty, I shone beyond the sun, it's been a long time, I was standing, damn, my dogs, the earth no longer carried me, and here I am at this hour: bones and stumps, a cursed cypress stripped bare, listen, I still hear the clamor of the chains, the hunt beating the bushes in the woods, the motor cut, the "Get out of the car, boy!" the Missing Person report, the rope of the grim reapers, the bodies never found, the bodies hunted, the bodies without, the bodies dangling from branches like pendants, listen, I know the stench and the sound of hate, I know men who sit in their office chairs, throats laughing, a whisky in their hand, listen, I have seen that and that too, the investigations, yeah right, the fabricated evidence, the evidence slipped in at the last minute, they burned the cars.

It was what it was. Barely out of the taxi, I was chatting with the neighbor, she was welcoming me, promising me that one of these days before the end of my stay we'd sit down together in her kitchen and try some of her cooking. Bag swung over my shoulder, I hung out on her porch. Chatted just to chat, and taking in the perfect symmetry of her dimples, the *popof* wrapped around her hair, and the oil-spattered apron, I thought about how good women like her have always been there, how there would always be houses open to strangers and the poor.

From my last name and something in my bearing, she gathered I was from Africa. I nodded without elaborating. What would Cameroon mean to anyone here? It was far away. Not one of her people knew where it was. Then things happened in quick succession: she handed me the keys and the cheap sheets that Denim, the owner of the rental, had left for me. She told me "That way," and I walked down a rutted alley into a tiny, unevenly paved courtyard to reach the coffin-with-a-window that I would occupy for the next six weeks. I didn't have the money to aim higher. What had gone for loose change before Hurricane Katrina, cost over a thousand dollars, ten years after. A shack now rented for the price of a palace. Cheap could no longer be found. That's why I hadn't tried to negotiate when Denim presented the price of this tourist rental in Tremé. She'd set the price at $800 a month and I'd taken it. Eight hundred in cash, plus deposit because it was furnished.

You could count the sticks of furniture on one hand. In the bedroom, its ceiling slung low, as if the sky had dozed off on top, nothing seemed built to last, except the sofa-bed. What a circus to pull it open! I laid down, fully dressed and wrung out. I'm no sophisticate. When I'm hungry, I eat, when I'm tired, I sleep. But not here. Here, the sandman ditched me. I rehashed my crossing all night long.

In Dallas, where I was supposed to catch a connecting flight to New Orleans, I'd followed the wrong signs, chased after shuttles that went nowhere, and rushed around for nothing, since I ended up at the check-in counter too late, and the next flight wouldn't leave until seven o'clock the next morning. Dog tired, I'd found something to revive me in an okay restaurant where the televisions and commercials weren't turned up full blast. There at Cousin's Barbecue in the airport, I got to chitchat with my first American Black.

Actually, it was Davis Rashad, plus a third name I've forgotten, who put himself out there first. Before learning how to stuff fries into cardboard containers, he'd been in trouble for some kind of non-payment. They'd taken his house, his TV, his car, his computers, everything but the Lord. They'd locked him up for five years in Louisiana State Penitentiary, which, before being a prison, had been a plantation. For two whole centuries it had produced sugar, tobacco, and coffee. Two centuries, that's a lot of Black men, most of them natives of Angola. Which explains the nickname. The prison was rechristened Angola. Davis, Rashad, etc., gave a quick chuckle, concluding, "This is a country that doesn't know forgiveness," a laugh that proved that everything was possible and painless in America, that what counted in the end, what would always boost a man to the rank of an American was the lessons he learned in life, experience. They said *life experience* like you would talk about a good life insurance policy or a profitable marriage contract backed up by a cartel of lawyers. Despite setbacks, cancers, and bankruptcies, they continued to believe in social self-redemption. They promised themselves to become better people.

When I saw his grandson's honor roll photo, I congratulated Davis. In return, because he was proud, Davis slid me an *uh huh* exactly like the one from the taxi driver at the airport in New Orleans, and from the neighbor woman in a head-wrap, the one charged with passing me the keys from the landlady, when I called to tell her I'd be late and arrive a day later.

Uh huh . . . exactly the same, then he swiveled forward on his hips to knock on the teak floor. It was a prayer to his god that misfortune spare the boy of his boy and go sleep in another room. Davis Rashad, etc., knew the statistics. When a Black American man reached his thirties without having festered in jail, they shouted, "Lucky man!" and toasted the miracle. Money and health came after.

So, I'd spent my first night in America in Dallas. In the taxi driving me to any cheap motel, I thought of the TV show that I'd been obsessed with as a teenager. I conjured up the Ewings and the Barneses, especially Cliff, the brother of JR's sister-in-law. Like my father, Cliff Barnes was the poor man in the show, he sweated poor, he cried poor, and if anyone put money in his hands, he devoured it quick-and-dirty like a poor man.

In the taxi, hurtling toward some bunkhouse in the Texan city, I assessed my motives for this trip. It had all started with an anecdote. When my brother Mathieu and I were having lunch at my mother's place, she'd brought up the memory of a relative we'd never heard about before. At some time in the past, from the home of *those other people*—my mother refused to refer to my father's family by their name—this man had gone off to seek his fortune in America. He'd boarded a cargo ship that shuttled between Douala and New Orleans. He'd stayed for about ten years in Louisiana, where he labored as a field worker on a plantation, then died in mysterious circumstances. According to some, for there are at least two versions to any story, they'd fished his rotted corpse out of a bayou. I'd wanted details. Louisiana is a big place, but my mother couldn't be bothered to provide answers, she was plagued by her tablecloth which we might mess up and by Mathieu's opinion of her veal filet.

And yet, that uncle had been the only one of his generation to leave. Like Jean Rouch's barefoot adventurers who go into the city in search of women and a few coins, he'd dreamed big. Not about Lagos or some other African megalopolis, but about the great West, this America that smelled so strong of hair conditioner that I almost gagged in the back seat of the taxi from the airport to the City of Dallas.

Etienne was his name. Etienne John Wayne Marie-Pierre. I had decided to make him my hero. He would eclipse my genitor. He would restore the pride that had been stolen from me. He would rid me of this *lack-of-being*, which had oozed inside me like an abscess for almost forty years, ever since we'd fled Yaoundé to live in Paris. I might have grown up, but I felt myself shriveling. I was being tainted by the past, and Jeanne had no idea.

Jeanne is my partner. For six years, we've been living in her apartment in the 12th arrondissement in Paris. We live among her knickknacks, her curtains, her furniture. We depend on her money, a teacher's salary. Once in a while, we travel, but this is the first time I've gone off without her.

In fact, it was the first time since we'd met that I expressed the need to go off on my own. Tactfully, I'd explained that this wasn't a vacation. I was going to New Orleans on a family pilgrimage and to revive my hope of writing a novel someday. The story of the great-uncle who had died in Louisiana would make a good subject. This last argument persuaded Jeanne, who continued to believe in my creative potential even though I had never in all my forty-nine years completed the slightest manuscript. My mother scolded me, of course. "Don't you have better things to do?" She was afraid I would end up like *him,* my father. She accused me of sponging off a woman who was too nice. I reassured myself by thinking back to my independent years, when, according to my brother, I'd had a knucklehead job in a bank and shown myself capable: car, rent, gadgets, stylish threads . . . I'd been able to buy myself all that.

I left anyway, with a pack on my back and a school notebook in which I'd scribbled what little I knew or surmised about the Cameroonian uncle in America. And now, here I was, in Tremé, my body laid out flat, feet pointing toward the screen door that dared to promise security when all the rest— the house, the poorly installed window, the rickety door handle—invited thieves to try their luck.

I had gotten up during the night to push the window all the way up to let in some air. Damned suffocating heat. Made me dizzy. I splashed cold water on my face and chest and stayed in bed until daybreak, my heart like a knot. I didn't know how this first day in town would be organized. Didn't have the heart to slog along on a schedule or the guts to venture out into the streets to confront the inevitable *what's the point?* that always hovers when you're traveling, when you've just unpacked your suitcase in a place you don't know. So, I spent the morning in my room and confined myself to fixing mechanical problems. I repaired the chain on the ceiling fan and switched it on and off a few times to fool myself into thinking I felt cooler. I fixed the pegs that held up the only shelf in the closet and stacked my clothes on it, methodically.

I'd packed a suit just in case, which I left in the garment bag and hung on a nail sticking out of the wall at an angle. In the microwave, which I scrubbed with a scratchy sponge, I reheated the sandwich left over from the airplane, then devoured it in bed as the afternoon faded to the patter of scattered footsteps outside, the aroma of sautéing onions, rice, and black-eyed peas. Outside, the air was scorching. Such heat in March was unusual, the neighbor had remarked, but people around here got used to anything.

I watched the grimy blades of the fan run in circles—they say it helps you sleep—and emerged twelve hours later on the wily bed that I gave up trying to fold and just shoved into a corner of the room. Through the double-hung window, I glimpsed a corner of the sky. It was the same stunning blue as the day before, the same old story. On a wire framed by two electrical poles, a row of unbeautiful birds chirped enough to get on my nerves.

I turned away from the window and looked warily at the narrow kitchen table and my notebook devoted to the uncle, along with two books on New Orleans and Louisiana. Jeanne had bought them for me as an apology. After I'd revealed my plan, and after she'd approved, she begged me to take her along. She'd help me with my research, we'd mosey through the streets at night, we'd gorge ourselves on jazz and victuals fit for a king, she wouldn't bother me since she'd only be staying a week. I said no. She was vexed: "I think it's strange that you insist on going alone."

Packing my bags that very night would have meant I was acting on instinct. Forget love. Instead, I just slept on my own side and woke up with Jeanne's plaintiff voice running through my head. What was so "strange"? That I was suddenly excited about a relative I'd never known, when I was no longer in contact with my father? That I was ready to sell the camera we'd bought for the fourth anniversary of our civil union to help finance my trip? That I was going off by myself to a city where more than half of the residents were black, and where more than half of those Blacks were women? I let the storm blow over and, as usual, Jeanne helped out a few weeks later, giving me the two tourism books and a plane ticket to New Orleans.

I stuffed the books back into my pack, feeling contrite. I was probably being selfish, fixating on myself. I grabbed my backpack and shoved it into the closet. I was far from home, far from my people, but their faces filled my mind too quickly. I had arrived in Tremé with all my hassles.

I was annoyed to hear the familiar ring of my phone, and slid it under the pillow, determined not to be there for anyone. It chimed again. The third time, I answered. My landlady was summoning me to her house.

* * *

It took me a while to find the house. Four times I walked past it before realizing that this house, portly as an embassy, this mass of bricks, wood, and ivy really was where Lisa Denim lived. The three-story Italianate structure had been built in

1857, shortly before the Civil War. Later, I learned that, in 1867, it had been sold at auction for seven thousand eight hundred dollars, then passed through the hands of about fifteen owners, both White and Black, before being purchased by Denim a few years before Katrina. The house had survived the hurricane but had grown irritable and fickle. When the wooden floors weren't crackling, it was the roof, the ceilings, the staircases, the plumbing.

I climbed the steps to the historic house, its front door standing open, and pulled on the doorbell. I heard a feeble jangle, and entered, coming into the kitchen where behind a marble counter a woman stood absorbed in preparing a vegetable smoothie. Clamped onto a small blender, she mixed pink with red, orange, and purple without lifting her eyes from the machine or bothering to greet me. I figured she was Denim by the way she finally laid her eyes on me. She wasn't looking at me, she was interested in pocketing my rent money and proving to herself that she ran her operation by the book. She accepted the photocopy of my ID card, had me sign two copies of a lease full of legalese, and slid the whole thing into the drawer of a breakfront cabinet that she locked with a key. After that, she grew a little more human, whipped me up a healthy smoothie and asked me what had brought me to the area. She expressed surprise that I wasn't in a position to rent a cottage. In her opinion, and she could only speak for herself, but in any case, it was a shame not to be able treat yourself as you grew older.

I admired the collection of masks hanging on the wall behind her. Most were from Africa and Indonesia. I also noticed a costume made of beads and feathers on display in a glass case, some orchids in a vase, art books on a pedestal table, a sculpture of a nude in the corner, pots and pans hanging overhead, two heads of Buddha, a live, flesh-and-blood cat on a chair, and produce stickers on the fridge: citrus fruit, carrots, and apples. Denim stroked her body almost as much as she did her money. Renting out hovels was not a calling. People needed her and she served people, simple as that. That's what she told me.

A man she called Josuah, who seemed to be her employee, walked in from outside carrying a toolbox. He was short, thick around the waist, had a small nose and thin legs. The top half of him disappeared under the sink to unclog the drainpipe trap. The bottom half that went from his knees to his shoes, seemed so frail, like two chicken legs. He climbed out again, tossed a clump of slime in the garbage and went out of the kitchen humming Sam Cooke. A CHANGE IS GONNA COME, it was soul music from the era of the Civil Rights movement that the little man was baritoning. It was my song. In my youth, I had listened to it with so much faith and fervor. I had trusted these lyrics announcing the end of oppression for the Black people of America and the entire world. I, a Cameroonian from France, I had totally gone with it.

I'd been twenty years old at the time and for me, African American artists were like so many Christs. Every record album, every book, every work they pulled from their gut sent me into a youthful frenzy. I refused to lend out my records and played them only when I was alone. I'd lock myself in the bathroom to recite passages of Baldwin that I'd learned by heart. I was obsessed by Black America. I was getting to be a jerk about it. But there was more. I felt like I hadn't grown up where you had to grow up to be a real Black man. Like I would always be too short, like I had plateaued at 5'10" and had no solid history behind me.

If my imported Black pedigree attracted certain women, I lost points whenever an African American showed up. Parisian women are romantics. Who wants to sleep with a guy from a village? In France, those Blacks were heroes. Crushing the Germans and fighting for their own emancipation on their soil made them forever beautiful. A Black man, I wanted to be one, too, so I could dream and draw strength. *Black is beautiful.* I would have sold my hide to be a child of Harlem.

A CHANGE IS GONNA COME. There, in the historic home, I closed my eyes to be lulled by the eternal promise and the voice of this gnome of a man with the ribcage of Goliath, that crazy ribcage that was probably his only fortune. I doubted that Denim's employee had such a huge house or car. When I opened my eyes, my landlady had left the room. A female figure was cleaning up the mess she'd left. The cat was circling the garbage can, meowing. The morning sunlight was streaming through the four windows, tall as church windows, and pouring across the ceiling encumbered with plaster molding.

I walked over to the bay window and looked out at the patio where bunches of white jasmine were blooming in a bathtub. Denim had bragged about them. Her house was the only one where the plants grew so well. Outside, on Governor Nicholls, a street whose name had changed many a time, most remarkable were the oak trees, older than the oldest families who lived there. Coming out of my room just a few minutes before, I had seen their extravagant roots buckling the sidewalk. Nature had battled here, and Black people, too. Born free or liberated from their chains, they had bought plots of land, built sturdy houses, businesses, and churches. They had made Tremé and they had lost it.

I recalled the taxi driver's well-crafted speech, the driver who had dropped me off in the quarter two days earlier, "Tremé is the Africa of America, we eat, we party, we dance, and we die like over there." However, seeing the neighborhood again this morning, congested with scaffolding and For Sale signs, I had the feeling of being not in Africa, not even in America, but on the edge of the world. I walked slowly, slowly to avoid tripping. I walked and visions of chaos layered atop reality. I imagined Tremé and the entire city swallowed up. Mud everywhere, the sky fallen, the earth broken. Every year, the water level rose. Every year, water threatened to drown everyone, just as it probably had Etienne John Wayne Marie-Pierre. Wandering the streets, I saw Katrina again, the water-logged earth and people searching for their dead. Some had never recovered the bodies, and for the stricken, the pain and rehashing would never end, they would never stop hearing the cries for help, or think they spotted a familiar ring or leg among the tattered rags and floating corpses. They would swear that Katrina was not just a hurricane, but a weapon against Black people and the poor. How else could you comprehend that a handful of experts, paid to manage the circulation of the waters, had chosen to leave such weakened levees in place? Somebody leaked a scandal about a plot involving explosives. Guys who had supposedly placed them all along the levees, and boom. A sinister hypothesis, and yet . . .

America is not Cameroon. At the time, coming across images of the catastrophe on television, I'd thought the houses would rise again, the corpses would be taken to the hospital and resuscitated, that people didn't die of hunger or fever or diarrhea or cholera in the place that had invented obesity, the Family Dollar store, take-out, the doggy bag, Black Friday, the FBI, Coca-Cola, and Malcolm X.

As I walked out of Denim's house, a truck full of men, bricks, and concrete blocks swept down Governor Nicholls Street. I stepped back to avoid being splashed by the vehicle, looked up, feeling droplets on my forehead. I hadn't seen the rain coming. It had been falling softly, already filling the holes in the poorly paved road. I saw more workers on the roof of a condominium. Hammering, all kinds of activity under a sky that was already clear, wide and hot again.

I spent the rest of the day stewing on my sofa-bed. My hand assaulting the flies. My eyes staring at the scaly wall separating the bedroom from the bathroom. My stomach was churning. Denim's vegetable smoothie was not sitting well. Even though I had downed an antacid as soon as I'd come back to the room. Even though I'd plastered my insides with the rice left next to the gas stove with its one functioning burner. I blinked away the sweat trickling into my eyes and glanced over at the faded yellow flowers on the fitted sheet. Forty-one more nights to get through, murmured my demons. I brushed them away, and pulled out the visiting card that Denim had given me.

The business card read Zaac the Handyman, and underneath the phone number was a picture of a man in a baseball cap and muscle shirt, brandishing his pecs and a masonry hammer. If everything he promised was true, there would soon be no more wrecked houses, or a single person without a roof in this town. This laborer also offered services as driver, tour guide, cook, carpenter, fisherman, mechanic, gardener, locksmith. He was a jack-of-all-trades and a child of the region. According to Denim who hired him from time to time, he would show me around and help me find information on my dead uncle. I swallowed another antacid, telephoned the laborer, and two hours later set off in his pick-up truck that was hardly more presentable than a garbage pail.

* * *

The day he was fired, Zaac gave up pampering his old tank. Losing a job, that can happen to anyone. What gnawed at him was his boss's contempt, his blackguard voice, the no-respect when he'd ordered Zaac to get out. Like putting chains on his ankles again, it was the same thing. "They cheated us then and they're cheating us still. They bait us like rats, break us like bricks, then they want an amen? They want me, Zaachary Ramses II, me, the flat-broke Black man standing before you, to pardon *them* and hand Obama another Nobel Prize? And how about my ass, while we're at it? Sorry, I don't play that game. I don't give a shit about peace."

From the moment he'd knocked on my door and made the sofa-bed creak by lowering all his weight onto it, I could find nothing to say or do in the face of this rage. It was the lot of the man and the country. It represented the Black man in America and I found it intimidating. To change the subject, I broached the question of finances. We needed to agree on a fee before we set out to do research. But Zaac had other priorities. "We'll figure it out later, Big Brother. First, we have to see if we can put up with each other. Who knows, I might have to shoot you before midnight." He tugged open the refrigerator door and jumped back like he'd seen the Devil: "What? There's nothing to drink at your house!" So, we were soon out rolling. Spitting his outrage between grievances, between curves in the road, we drove on with Zaac harping, "They cheated us . . . "

Clouds big and fat plastered the horizon. Out the window, the sky was descending. The faster we drove, the more the city looked like an island, enclosed, encircled by mist and detached from the mainland. In the streets, men wavered like shadows. I could no longer make out the sidewalk, or the haloes around the streetlights or the stars. Everything ran together like in a dream.

We parked the pick-up and I followed Zaac down to the marina. His eyes were wide open, the Mississippi like a TV screen with blinking lights that signaled passing ferries. "See how fast they go?" said Zaac picking up a pebble and aiming it at the red-and-blue reflections. They swept past, as if bragging, and Zaac's only retort was to fling pebbles at them.

As the mist lapped up the boats, I asked Zaac where they were headed. Zaac dropped his last pebble on the embankment. "I hope they're going to hell!" He stared at the point on the river where the last skiff had disappeared.

In a Richard Wright novel, two Black boys sit motionless, watching the city live and breathe, the city of Whites that has rejected them. They will never be part of it and they know it. That same powerlessness was making Zaac's head explode, that same feeling of being kept out of the game. "I used to have a boat, too. I used to go out fishing with my buddies. It was cool." He'd bought a barbeque grill and on weekends, when he felt like it, he'd grill hotdogs and ribs for everyone.

We stood there for a time, then went to a bar where women hung out. Nothing but women on the dance floor. Outside in the parking lot, men were peeling out in their cars. Others were stringing bets together and slamming glasses on the counter. We ordered beers and liquor and sat down at a table over by the jukebox. The only music Zaac cared about was the music of New Orleans, created by and for New Orleanians. He had enough quarters in his pocket to take over the machine at the bar and monopolize it for the whole evening. He selected twenty songs that I could only half-hear, since he gave a lecture on every song as it pulsed, telling me what it was about and who had written it. For his money, Buddy Bolden, the cornet player, was still the best. Zaac mimicked him, blowing out his cheeks, then tapping his temple because the artist had ended his days in an insane asylum in Jackson.

Transported by the Jelly Roll Morton blues celebrating Bolden, Zaac lifted his body to swing. His moves were graceful, his step agile. Surprising for a man so loaded with alcohol. He tossed me a *Come on*, which I brushed away with a little wave of refusal. When he insisted, I looked the other way. I wasn't sure I still knew any moves. Even though I used to be a pretty good reveler. I even knew the killer steps.

I uncapped a bottle of beer with a knife point and poured a glass for myself right to the top. The Andygator wasn't cold-cold, but at least it was local. It's a beer that every man should taste before he dies, declared the fix-it man, who was still out on the dance floor. He was now dancing with a girl who seemed to be to his taste, judging by the way his eyes were peeling her like a piece of fruit. Actually, he wasn't staring at her, so much as at her translucent white skin. I watched Zaac probe her skin and tried to read the look in his eye. He was thinking of the young woman's mother, the shame this mother would have felt if she'd happened to be at this den at the same time as us—she, the American of an America that had forbidden mixed marriages and cut everything in two: buses, schools, public buildings, public johns, neighborhoods. The shame felt by these women is what had turned men into wild beasts.

The girl acted like she was enjoying herself, but she was clearly a little afraid. Not afraid of Zaac as Zaac, but Zaac as local Black man. I watched Zaac's eye follow the path of her blood as it flowed under her pale skin. It was the exceptionally fine blood of Southern mothers flowing through her, not just red but dark and sticky. It wasn't blood that you staunched with black pepper or a tourniquet when it bled. No, you called the doctor or a priest. A blood tough as leather which, having survived over time and believing in its own purity, did not mix well. That's why the little thing was mixing in this bar where no mother had ever set foot.

From my table where the beer cans were piling up, I watched her trying her best. I could understand and excuse her. She wasn't *my* White girl, and I wasn't Zaac. Her mother had never insulted me. Her father had never hanged me or set me on fire. All that was Zaac's history. To each his own persecutors. To each his own ghosts. My own memory of Whites had started and ended in Cameroon.

There are some memories that cut you to the core. My heart had internalized a slew of them in my childhood, scenes of daily life in Yaoundé where, protected by his skin and showy eyeglasses, an ill-dressed Frenchman, an Italian, a Brit, or a German sped around in a garish SUV spewing exhaust fumes through the unfinished streets of the city. When he parked and when he got out, you had to see his impeccable arrogance, chomping on his gum, patting his wallet to make sure it was still there, rushing into the supermarket built for the nouveaux riches where employees greeted him with "Good Day, Mister White Man! How are you doing, Mister White Man?" And his arrogance as he barely acknowledged the employee, then barely tipped another who, after loading his groceries into the trunk, guided him, gesticulating theatrically, as he backed his SUV out of the parking space.

The worst was when *monsieur* assumed the fake smile of the repentant, and oozing with indulgence, financed a neighbor's Tabaski, paid an insane sum to maids who stole his shirts, attended weddings and baptisms when invited, said "Bonjour, how's the family?" in the vernacular, and paraded around in a pagne on Independence Day.

I had dealt with my first real White man at the age of eight. I hated him, I hated them all. I would have loved to scrape them right off the land, like you scrape the lard off a block of rillettes. Mop the floor with the face of that French lycée principal who had lived in my hometown for seventeen years, married to a local woman. He was so happy with his light-brown doll-baby that he'd bought her a convertible and made her secretary. "Secretary, where? You guessed it, secretary at the Hilton Hotel!" This was my mother's refrain: "The kind who takes her fanny up to the hotel's top floor because she has a continental figure."

I had never set foot in the Yaoundé Hilton, but in my child's mind, coming from a Catholic family of modest means, I imagined a harem for rich people, movie stars, and foreigners. They went in dressed to the nines and ended up buck naked on Asian rugs and all the rest that my limited experience and biases let me conjure up. But my mother, who was employed as an English teacher at the high school, attacked again, and with a handful of words, a few new juicy tidbits, transformed the grandiose into something sordid. She launched into gossip and *bam*, it all came tumbling down. The top floor of the five-star hotel metamorphosed into a corner grocery, and the most gorgeous babes in the world turned into fish heads. In Yaoundé, a "fish head" was like a "luxury prostitute," but more graphic and so much more vivid that it took me twenty years to respect a woman's beauty.

Whenever I waited for my mother inside the guarded gate at the French high school, I hoped to catch sight of the car and the Fish Head. I had only ever run across them together one time and was gobsmacked. The lady and her convertible were exactly alike: fast and refined. One day, when my mother was late picking me up, I saw the Hilton lady get out of her red car. She wasn't at the wheel, she was being driven by her husband, the boss, a guy not well built, who didn't even talk to her, didn't even smile at her, didn't even have the decency to admit that without his money and his value—thanks to his color—he couldn't have spent a single moment by her side. That day, it was like all the heat in the city went to my head. Not just the sun, but also the little people who work in it: the ones who lay bricks, who patch, who sweep the streets in front of the embassies to keep things clean as a whistle . . .

In short, it was all boiling over inside my head. When the convertible stopped to let me cross the street, I spit on it.

The story could have ended there. The headmaster could have cursed me and disappeared. But my mother, who had watched the whole scene from a distance, arrived at a run, grabbed me by the ear, and ordered me to apologize. She was afraid of losing her job at the school. She was setting aside a little money each month to leave the house, the country, and my father. Swallowing your anger is not just an expression, it's also physical. It involves your throat, your stomach, your whole body. It hurts, it makes you cry. It becomes entrenched, and the scar doesn't heal. For my mother, I swallowed my anger. I apologized to the White man and the other woman, who had jumped out of the sports car to insult me. "Don't you dare touch our car with your filthy hands." She was treating me like a beggar and a son of the whore that she herself was. I was sure of it now.

The car took off. I just stood there on the asphalt with our humiliation and my mother way out ahead of me. I watched her hand that never had enough reach up to flag a shared taxi. My father had gambled away our bicycle. Her jaw was tight. My mother sucked on her teeth until we fled from Cameroon, my mother, me, and my soon-to-be-born brother. I left my country feeling like a dog, my heart laden with my mother's bitterness and my own child's rage.

Zaac brought his American woman over to the table. He raised his bottle and gave a toast to the 1950s. He hadn't been alive at the time but it seemed like he had. What his father, born in 1940, told him had made such an impression that he used *I* instead of *he*. "I lived in a brick house and got up at four in the morning to earn my dollars. When I started my job as a shoeshine, they paid me a nickel. I always wore a shirt and bowtie. Barracks Street, where I grew up, had been slave quarters."

"To the Good Ol' Days!" he shouted, sending a glass of Moonchild down his gullet. And we repeated, I repeated "To the good ol' days," while his lady, eyeing the bottom of her glass, latched onto the legend of her great-great-grandfather who had made himself with his own hands. It was quite something for a man with no personal fortune to purchase a farm in Mississippi and plant cotton and rice. He had certainly earned people's pride in him, they cited him as an example and celebrated him as a saint. How many times had she heard this ancestor's name? Every single day, since everything her family owned bore his name. She counted them on her fingers: Rheedes Lake, Rheedes Cottage, Rheedes Farm, Rheedes Luxury Limousine, Rheedes Health Insurance, Rheedes Funeral Home, Rheedes Market, Rheedes School, it was dizzying. How many Zaacs, how many Zaac arms had Rheedes worn to a stub to enrich himself? She had no idea. She'd had nothing to do with it. She swirled the liquor in her glass.

"Make her dance! Make her dance, for godsake!" Zaac whispered to me, as he crushed a couple of cockroaches that were skittering across the table. His jaw was clenched. His eyes were rolling around in their sockets as he rubbed his fingers convulsively on the kneepads of his denim overalls. Was there any Black man on this earth more screwed than the Black man in America? Was the game rigged against anyone's fate more than his? Was any position more dicey than the one that this country reserved for him?

I stood up to invite the little lady to dance. I drank like a tourist, and then woke up in my bedroom the next morning with strings of plastic beads around my neck.

In the bathroom, with the door locked, I could see that only my mustache and my high forehead really belonged to me. The rest I owed to my people. I had my mother's skin and wrinkles. Suddenly, I felt exhausted, like an old lady. I removed the strings of beads and ran a bath. In Paris, I almost never took a bath, afraid that Jeanne might see me as lazy and view as abnormal and worrisome my status as ex-bank employee in search of a job. To prove that I had drive, I had given up a whole list of little domestic pleasures. No more sleeping in during the week, no more spending the whole day in pajamas, no more drinking beer before noon. In return, she left me alone. Jeanne believed in me and defended me every time her father subjected me to one of his interrogations or served me one of his lectures. He called me "mon p'tit gars" and saw himself as a hero.

I slid down into the warm water, and with great effort pulled my knees up to my chest and suds-ed up my cheeks where whiskers were already sprouting. Darn. I thought of the Philips razor I'd forgotten in the Dallas motel and the *No beard* rule that I had doggedly enforced all my life to keep my hairy father at a distance, to prohibit him, expel him from my body where he kept invading, like a dandelion in a square of lawn. I dug out my tweezers and a mirror to rid myself of the most visible hairs. Of all the trifles a man might have to deal with in the morning, plucking hairs was the worst. I worked on them for just a couple minutes, then sank back down into the clawfoot bathtub. My head felt dull, my body leaden from jetlag, and half of Sunday still loomed.

I stared up at the ceiling that was twice as high as in the room where I slept. Denim had installed a fake crystal chandelier that threw too little light to be practical. Aside from the chair that was serving as a soap dish, I couldn't see the décor clearly. The varnished cypress floorboards gave the room a fantastical appearance, the illusion of being on a stretch of heavy black water. The bathtub was my canoe, and I was gliding along.

To be honest, I could have stayed there until evening, waiting for Zaac to come back and chat or simmer, and take me out to one of those bars where the only real fight he was sure to win was the one he started. To be honest, I could have gone through the same conversations, hit the same clubs, danced the same dances, then come back to this room that was so dark that you had to turn on the lights at noon to see anything. Or I would have done the opposite: hope for nothing, not move, submit to this city they called the *Big Easy*, probably because it made you soft and lazy. Lulled by the water, I felt sleep taking over. Seriously, I would have fallen asleep if

Mary, the woman from next door with her *popof*, hadn't knocked at the door.

An hour later, I offered her a bottle and made my way into her kitchen where a crush of housewives was hard at work as though preparing to feed the entire state of Louisiana. She introduced me: "He's the African." I returned the smiles and shook hands, wondering, asking her with a masculine start that was just shyness, where the men were. She led me through a room where three boys, maybe ten years old, were mimicking the choreography of a video clip on TV. In the next room, cramped and dimly lit, a human shape lay spread-eagle on a broken-down bed. I paused in front of the feet with cracked skin that were poking out from under the *patchwork*—or "quilt," as they say here. They looked like a pair of old clod-hoppers you might see at a flea market. Inevitably, they brought thoughts of death.

I looked away, thrown off by these houses with rooms that spooled out one after the other. At home, people locked their bedroom door. Listening at the door was considered nosy. I had never walked in on my mother in her nightgown.

I came out into the backyard where a bunch of guys built like armoires were sitting in a circle on plastic chairs, drinking beer and relaxing. One of them, Mary's boyfriend, was trying to cook some ribs. The ribs were still not cooking, as the grill was not performing. Without irritation, he added more charcoal, turned the meat over, and lit a cigarette that he came over to smoke by me. Behind the odor of tobacco, I detected cologne that he had dabbed on his temples. His short-sleeved shirt faded by the sun was tucked into jeans. A carabiner holding about twenty keys dangled from one of the belt loops. He kept stroking the keys with his thumb. He was in his sixties, but his beer belly and bushy gray mustache seemed to add years.

"Having a good time?" I acted cheerful and we managed to tug on a thread of conversation, only half of which I could follow as my migraine had kicked in again. I felt it intensify as Paul, his first name was Paul, grew increasingly affable, poured his heart out to me. After telling me about his oldest daughter's wedding and some time spent in Africa years ago, forever ago, while he was in the Navy, he spoke proudly about playing a role in the TV series *Tremé* for two seasons. The series had ended, and some movies had been filmed in the area, but given the toll taken by all the energy required for the on-site work . . . Clearing his throat, he pointed at the little wooden house standing at the back of the yard. Still needed to put a lot of sweat into the shotgun before it would be able to house tourists. The roof was bald of shingles, and the walls were begging for resurrection, with half the clapboards cracked or swollen with rain. As for the 15' x 30' swimming pool, Mary's dream, that would have to wait a few months, until the rains had passed.

Paul sighed and laid his hand on the breast pocket of his shirt, that is, over his heart. "I am the best carpenter in New Orleans", which he pronounced *New Waaall'inz*, stretching out the second syllable. "I was born here, *uh*, went to school here, *uh-huh*, buried my mother here, married a girl here, *uh*."

The interjections came from the guys on the plastic chairs, not out of habit but to signify their solidarity with their host. What he declared they could affirm. Paul palavered and they were the chorus. A collection of tenors and basses, whatever, they were tuned and triumphant, singing their pride in sustaining a community and their pride in resisting, with no weapons beyond love and tradition in a society where "every home is a castle and every man for himself" was gaining ground.

I turned around. They were behind us, nodding in time, their chairs arranged in an arc. The only thing missing was a shade tree, an assortment of *boubous*, and the haunting twang of a stringed instrument to convince me that we were in Northern Cameroon, on the outskirts of Garoua. We had family there, I could see them in my mind's eye, relaxed on their mats at the foot of a cashew-nut tree and eating what there was to eat: mangos, rice, fish pulled from the river and smoked.

And the music. My mother had a cousin, a balafon player, who'd cut two records and made a successful debut in France and Germany in the 1960s. From that experience, he'd gained immeasurable self-love, affirming, "I'm a genius," opening his eyes wide. They were outlined with pencils sold two-at-a-time by Indian merchants. He was off for his ten minutes of fame. Charles Aznavour and James Brown stole his pieces. He'd been too much of a sucker to believe that those stars who weren't even stars would not give him credit. Only once did a newspaper cite his name. The article was short, but he'd had it framed and showed it to his audience before every solo performance.

So, the cousin was always part of the gatherings, and on our visits to the North, he invariably took his place in this courtyard, dressed like a star in an outfit unadapted to the climate. He had a soft spot for leather and plastered his body with it: boots, shirt, hat, half-finger gloves, necktie, and those odd chaps that cowboys wear when riding horseback. He played the role all the way, interspersing his pieces with anecdotes and reflections that thrilled the audience and earned him cheers. The *uhs* flowed naturally. Brotherly *uh-huhs* reflecting our connections in a concrete way.

Forty years after Garoua, I was alone among strangers, the only one to stay silent as Paul, upheld by his people, spoke about his life and imagined his death. "When I'm gone," he began, now solemn, lowering his head and peeking up at us, a look acquired through his acting experience, "don't lay my name and my shadow down far from here *huh*. Wash my body *huh* Take me to the church *huh* Sing for me, walk me *huh* And let my spirit go *huh*, Let it go let it go let it go . . ."

I was disarmed by these giant men, brothers in their jeans, molded by an energy that went back deep in time. Had this force preceded the great scattering? Had it started with the opening of the ship holds when they'd had to endure the rope and the slice of the whip, the stinging ants that haunted the wounds, when men, women, and children, jostled about worse than dogs, had to break their back and bloody their hands picking cotton? When they'd had to survive, in any case, and on Sunday, every Sunday, let go together, share their sorrows and metamorphose them into collective laughter.

Paul laughed, everyone threw back their head and laughed, except me, still in the vise of my migraine and powerlessness to rally with the group. I no longer knew how to share. Away from Garoua and Yaoundé, I had grown into a man without people, severed from my life force. In Paris, my mother had pushed Cameroon and our life from before into a corner. She kept telling me "A man is not a plant, he can grow anywhere." It was a lie. How could we get along without our community? And when I heard her get up during the night and pace up and down in our rabbit cage, when I listened to her rifling through the cupboards in search of something sweet to wolf down with no appetite and no time to sit down, I called out to her, begged her to come into my room and hug me tight. I prayed for our family to be whole again. For years, I prayed to Mary for this.

I tore myself away from these painful memories and watched the cooks stream into the backyard here in Tremé with steaming platters. Little girls followed on their heels. One of them, who had long, black hair, scampered over to snuggle in Paul's arms. Her green eyes shaped like dugout canoes inspected me with the self-possession of a budding show-off, one who will never question her own beauty. She already had what black women dream of when they feel alienated: light skin and hair that flowed freely. She continued studying me but spoke to Paul.

"Is this man really from Africa?"

With my striped shirt buttoned up to my neck, my clean-shaven face, controlled afro, fanny pack over my shoulder, and the flat, labored English that came out of my mouth, I probably didn't conform to the distorted image of the African continent that a middle-schooler in the United States might hold. In her mind, Africa was a skeleton with a hand perpetually out-stretched toward the West.

When I explained that I lived in Paris, that did pique her interest. She turned to face me and boasted of having Europeans among her ancestors. "Janet's family is an old Creole family," Paul explained, pulling the overcooked ribs off the fire and depositing them on a platter of sautéed sweet potatoes. "If you saw her Great Aunt Brenda, you'd probably take her for a White woman. And if you saw her sister Edna, you'd never believe that both of them came out of the same belly. She's black-black, like I am. Genetics, it's beyond our understanding."

I knew about African albinos and Antillean chabins, but light-skinned Blacks, ultra-light to the point of passing for White, I'd only come across those reading Faulkner. Paul gave me a wink that I would only understand later, and waited for the budding show-off to scamper away, before telling me the history of these descendants of Africans and Europeans. Some of them who came out of the womb so white, they chose to pass for White. They'd been a Louisiana specialty still alive and well at the time of Janet's great-aunt. Some had migrated to other states, to a place where nobody knew them, so that they could recreate themselves and claim that they were White.

Paul's wink was intended to tell me that Brenda was one of those. Typical, one hundred percent, with silky hair, white flesh on her cheeks. And a deep-rooted desire to gain access to the forbidden White world. In 1951, with all that plus stockings, three hats, a shirtwaist dress, and high-heel pumps, she had set out for Pittsburgh.

Paul, inexhaustible, portrayed the kind of life that Brenda had led in minute detail. No longer was she Brenda, he now called her "Ehren Jenson's wife," Jenson being the local industrialist who had married Brenda, not suspecting her origins.

Ehren Jenson's wife's masked balls, Ehren Jenson's wife's fur stoles, diamonds, and porcelain china, Ehren Jenson's wife's cook, maid, chauffeur, all of them Black for sure . . . Paul described it all to me as I sat there, bobbing my head like a plastic dashboard bulldog. "Genetics, it's beyond our understanding," he repeated, pulling his chair up close to mine and leaning heavily on the back. He was finally coming to the epilogue.

From 1952 to 1955, Brenda Ehren Jenson led an exemplary life, giving birth to two white babies. But things soured when the third child was born, when it came out and she saw his color. Paul insisted, as if he'd been right there in the bedroom in Pittsburgh, that Brenda screamed "Black!" A *black* so monumental that Ehren threw his wife out of the house. All night long, Brenda wandered the streets, bellowing, then sought refuge in a church, trailing the dirty, scandalous body. For a long time, she would be surprised that no shock had registered on the babe's face, no anger, no chagrin when she abandoned him. In short order, Brenda returned to the South to live with her mother, where she was still, knitting baby blankets and little onesies. She'd never seen her children again. "It's something beyond our understanding. Thank God times have changed."

Now that she had finished stuffing herself with beignets, Janet clapped her hands to call for silence, then launched into a song like the ones that children intone on festival days at school. At the chorus, two girls with curly brown hair popped out from under a table to join in. They disappeared again, when the applause intended for Janet began, and it occurred to me that the world had not changed, the world was still organized like a plantation where it was the bastards and bitches who thrived.

* * *

As I peeled my thighs off the plastic chair seat, I noticed that the courtyard had emptied out. Only Paul and a trio of drunks were still hanging around, deep in a debate for and against Obama. In the kitchen where a young girl was filling Tupperware containers with rice and ribs, Mary was scrubbing dishes and muttering, "Black people are flesh-and-blood people. Not saints." She supported Obama and blamed his opponents, and among them the most pissed his body about to tip over, was threatening to fight to defend what he called true democracy.

Their voices filtered through Governor Nicholls Street, which I was now trudging down, as if to tame the hours separating me from morning, and contain the nausea I felt coming on again, as my shadow spread across the pavement. There was a full moon, not the ideal time to land in the ill-frequented streets of Clairborne, North Clairborne Avenue, where the worst could befall you, where people beat up other people, where people sometimes killed other people for less than a handbag. The day I'd arrived, someone had stabbed someone else, someone had stolen somebody's car, someone had broken into somebody's house to rob it. I got this information from Zaac who got it from Crime Alert, a site he subscribed to so he wouldn't hold illusions about the society he lived in. Zaac's telephone shrieked every time blood flowed somewhere or some ugly event happened in New Orleans. His phone might screech several times in a single night. Zaac would jump on it to find out who, how, and where and to make sure none of his crew was in danger.

I tightened my grip on the shoulder strap of my fanny pack containing passport, cell phone, and a few dollars, then slowed my pace when I caught sight of two individuals posted on the sidewalk a few yards ahead. I hesitated to turn around or step up my pace toward the red light and finally decided to just keep moving, cursing my carelessness and my too-visible bag. What was I thinking, going out with a bag like this? Why would I think I should be walking through a city where almost everyone went by car?

I had panicked for nothing. As I walked past, the men greeted me and wished me a good trip home, by which they meant "safe." I told them that I was staying not far from there and asked them out of curiosity where this road led. Surprised, one of them told me that it led to the cemetery, at least at this hour, at least for a man out all alone. Beyond the stop light, under the bridge, was another world. A ghetto of tarps, oil drums, and desperate people living off crime and begging. In that abyss, situated under the city, so to speak, a boy had been found, his body chewed up by an ax. The man who hadn't said anything leaned back and swallowed. "If you have God in your head, nothing can hurt you." He'd served in Haiti, Iraq, and Somalia. Compared to here, it was hell, yet he'd come back to this country on his two feet. I thanked him for the advice, doubled back the way I'd come and telephoned my partner Jeanne, whom I hadn't called a single time since my arrival.

Five days with no call, no text, no email, that was too much! Jeanne's voice was dry as the bell ending school recess. She had imagined scary scenarios. Much longer, and she would have been en route to Louisiana.

I listened as her breathing slowed and she settled her behind in a seat. I imagined her sitting there, legs crossed too high for 6:42 a.m., presiding in our custom-built kitchen, a gift from her parents. I apologized because I had to, but I failed to explain my silence. The truth is that I hadn't felt the need to hear her voice. The truth is that I was no longer in love. I still loved her, but mostly out of habit. I'd grown used to her breasts, her scent, her texture, her turns of phrase. It all came back to me automatically when I was far away, without evoking any new or strong emotion in me. "That's taken care of," I told myself each morning as I woke up on my side of the conjugal bed. "No need to look any further, my friend." We were a couple with domestic habits and morals.

So, out of loyalty and out of principle, I let Jeanne pull me back into the world I had just left. It was going to be a lousy spring in France this year, a brewery had opened just down the street from us, my mother had called, I'd received a letter from the Unemployment Office, the washing machine was working again, Jeanne had gone to the hairdresser. That was good news, I said, because I loved to hold the back of her neck when we kissed. Her voice softened. I hung up and rushed out into the tiny courtyard adjacent to my bedroom, and found a note signed *Ramses II the Great*.

Zaac wanted to introduce to me someone who worked at a plantation. He called her "the phone book" because she knew so many things and so many people. The plantation was located near Baton Rouge. We'd go there early next week. We'd leave at dawn to avoid getting heat stroke.

I wrapped myself up like a mummy to sleep but didn't drop off until the first rays of dawn. Same thing the next day and the days that followed. This is how it had been every night since I'd arrived in the city. When I got up in the morning, it was like hauling my body up from the depths of a well. Something in the air didn't agree with me. I woke up bathed in sweat, then a second later was shivering. I felt groggy, I felt feverish.

During these days that loomed like mountains, making regular calls to Jeanne ended up helping me kill time. I told her things about my old uncle and New Orleans, stories I inflated, since I barely ever left my shack.

* * *

The day of our trip to Baton Rouge, I caught sight of my landlady as I was settling into Zaac's pick-up truck. She was coming out of her house, wheeling a suitcase. Besides Zaac, the oak trees, and me, she was surely the only one out this hour. The only person in the neighborhood decked out in a linen suit, high-heel platform shoes, and a big shaggy silver-gray head of hair. iPhone wedged between her cheek and shoulder, she strode imperiously toward her Pontiac, while Zaac, instead of starting up his truck, observed her in his rearview mirror, shaking his head.

He still couldn't get over the fact that Denim paid a coach and made the rounds of the biggest poker tournaments in the country with the hope of hitting it big. "Next time, I'm gonna get that ring!" That's what she vowed every time she came back from one of her trips. She dreamed of making it to the finals so she could win that diamond ring. She dreamed of being even richer and making a place for herself among the phallocrats and racists. Denim claimed to be the only Black woman in America to shine at poker.

Zaac explained how the two worked, the country and Denim. There was no plain old *being* in America, there was only financial being. That was born when you started working and got your American Social Security number. Then there was your credit score, which was variable. It evolved depending on your job and what you did with your money or how you frittered it away. The more you paid off debts quickly and completely, the higher your score climbed, the more the banks loved you, and the more your financial being was enhanced. On the other hand, the opposite happened if you accumulated too many late payments. No more loans or credit cards for you, you fell into disgrace and no longer existed.

Thus, there was nobody more American than Denim, and nobody more clever than the Denims of the world who, early on, had grasped one simple fact: everybody, at some point, dies and has to be buried. And so, since 1846, the Denims had been helping their fellow citizens put their people into the ground. They were Number One in the city. Their services ranged from embalming the body to organizing the jazz funeral, which my guidebook described as *a musical funerary tradition born in New Orleans*, and which cost a pretty penny. As if, aligning itself with the ever-increasing cost of living, death had no scruples about raising its price.

Zaac was horrified by at the insane price of a coffin and the high cost of a funeral. I was listening distractedly, haunted by all the living people I had so far encountered who looked like the walking dead, Blacks with morose features, sitting or standing as they waited for the bus. Twenty-year-olds looked like thirty-year-olds, thirty-year-olds like forty-year-olds, and forty-year-olds looked like grandfathers. Which they were, for the most part, actually, since their daughters had babies early.

In the bus, which I'd taken twice, a lot of the passengers dozed, taking advantage of a reasonably clean seat, a quiet corner to begin or round out their night. In the bus, some of them rummaged through plastic shopping bags containing a bit of laundry or medications with no packaging, or bills. Where would they get off the bus? Where would they rush to after this vehicle, chilly as a morgue, had tossed them out onto a highway for large vehicles? I'd felt ill-at-ease among them.

A failure, the lady loaded down with children and Family Dollar purchases and focused on trying to open two cans of soda without spilling them all over her thighs, this lady whose belly protruded too far to button her shorts. Surprised by my accent, she asked me in an English that revealed a lack of any valid financial being where I was from and why I was here. She meant *in this hole*, this South where there was nothing for *us*. I stammered *good luck* as I got off the bus and missed the bottom step, I was so pressed to be beyond the reach of these poor people I wasn't treating like brothers. I couldn't bring myself to say, "What's up, bro?" when I saw a man of my color. I had stopped dreaming and was beginning to feel shameful relief at not being them, not being mistaken for them.

After the Family Dollar woman, I was in a state of rage against the poor Blacks and all the Whites in the South. In my bedroom where I had come back to lie down, I thought— and God, I was so ashamed to feel it so strongly—"I can be Black anywhere: in South Africa, Namibia, Togo, the Antilles,

Cuba . . . But the worst of the worst is being Black in the United States. It means being potentially guilty and historically wretched. I don't want to grow old in prison because I've been transformed into a dealer, a wife beater or a vagrant. I don't deserve to end up ignorant and obese."

I chewed on these thoughts until morning, when it was blustering and storming with such fury that the trees and telephone poles were swaying. Then the city calmed down. The neighbors brought out coolers full of beer. They hadn't even stirred from their porches.

Denim got out of her Pontiac and waved in our direction. Zaac grumbled and I understood that we would not be going to Baton Rouge. He was already climbing out of the pick-up truck to get his butt over to her. Aside from his gift for gab, he did not have the bearing of a pharaoh. A few moments later, he reappeared and summed up the situation. For reasons that were none of his business, Denim's tournament had been canceled. "So, we've got her on our back," he said, scratching his behind and getting back into the truck. "She wants me to go to Hammond to run an errand for her. She says it can't wait. What can you do? That's women, for you."

I slid my sunglasses back on, grabbed my bag from the back of the pick-up, and paused before crossing the street to greet Denim, the boss lady of all the workers. Governor Nicholls Street was now wide awake: neighbors, workers, churchgoers, garbage trucks . . . I stood there on the sidewalk gandering, disoriented by this day that seemed to be starting up for everyone but me. Timidly, I waved to Mary who was out sweeping in front of her shotgun house and glimpsed Paul's figure in front of the TV that was already lit. From here, I could hear the lively voices of the announcers who had probably slept well, breakfasted well, done everything well that people do when they understand that life is slipping past.

Denim got back into her car and waved me over. She had taken off her blazer and high heels to drive. She offered to take me with her to see a friend. "Yes, or no?" She was leaving now. I glanced over at Mary, who was just shutting her front door again. In the alley that separated my room from another house, equally dilapidated, a young woman was hanging bedsheets out to dry. At seven o'clock in the morning, the sun was already slapping her head.

I sank into the cool passenger seat in Denim's car with a fake-cool grin. Denim adjusted the air conditioning and we drove over to Bywater, where Zona lived.

It was after Katrina that Bywater had become Bywater— a neighborhood structurally white, thick with hipsters, and with no whiff of utopia but with a high level of cultural and economic capital. They were sons of rich bastards, who devoted themselves to experiences: purifying their body with Detox Juices, moving house by bicycle because it's more ecological, getting a tattoo on their calf that said *I like a lady with a mustache*, wearing skirts without shaving their legs, skinny dipping in the Country Club swimming pool, learning Contact Improvisation, communicating with their ancestors and asking them to bless the house they owned. Zona presided over these last two sectors, and for the past seven years had enjoyed the title of priestess.

She dressed accordingly. Never pants or factory-made clothes; instead, ankle-length, hand-sewn dresses that came from Benin, Port-au-Prince, or Bahia. Never sneakers or closed-toe shoes; instead, sandals, so her toes could breathe. And her hair? Hard to say, since her head was wrapped as tight as a sausage.

In a city where voodoo priestess Marie Laveau the Elder was still venerated, where 133 years after her death, people still left all kinds of stuff on her grave—hair, fingernails, bones, etc.—Zona's career had taken off easily. In just one month, her name and phone number had made the rounds of every neighborhood. People addressed her with deference and only showed up at her house when the divinities she served had so decided. Hence, there were certain days when you could go to Zona's house, and other days when she was not to be disturbed. When she spoke, you had to keep quiet and listen as if dumbstruck, to her talk about the countries where she'd been to *connect* with her African ancestors.

She received us dressed in orange and yellow, in homage to a divinity that was crazy about these two colors. She showed me around her house, a New Age bazaar, outfitted for ceremonies and religious rituals. Her bedroom was dedicated to the natural spirits and to Yemanja, the water goddess of African origin whose double was called Olokun and whose children were fish.

After sprinkling drops of alcohol on the dining-room floor, Zona filled our glasses and our plates, then went on about an exhibition of traditional African art that she had just visited at the NOMA. In detail, she described the masks, the *récades*, statuettes made of nails, while Denim droned a string of *amazing*s and *awesome*s, not even listening.

I concluded that they were crazy. Especially Zona, Giant Zona, for she had to be 6'6", was homesick for Africa, which for her meant a paradise with wise men on street corners, altars in every hut, spirits in every tree trunk and in every body of water. Even though, the only part of the continent that she had ever seen was the airport in Cotonou and the Door of No Return on the beach at Ouidah. She had read through *Flash of the Spirit* by Robert Farris Thompson, and the knowledge that she'd drawn from it had helped her become guest speaker at conferences, where she began her speeches with "We, the Africans of America."

The magus disappeared, leaving me alone in the living room. Denim was out on the balcony, online with her friend Angeleta who was telling her about a ball for the local Black notables who fought over invitations to attend. The issue wasn't who could pony up the 500 bucks to get in, but rather who had not received an invitation at all. In other words, who was a loser. Next, the two gossips fulminated against Owens Astorga, the lawyer who had offered Angeleta four dinners and two nights in a hotel while also dating someone else. Angeleta suspected that he was still going out with Liberty's sister Kristin. Denim had no opinion on this, so she assessed his fortune instead. This guy didn't wait until the end of the month to make money, she insisted. "He is money. He's a strong man."

Internally, I lamented the insipidness of the hunt for women, based on the same rules, no matter who you were or where you came from. To conquer, a man had to be positioned to invest in gasoline, living expenses, maybe even flowers. I counted up the number of bouquets and weekends I had offered in my life. What did people say about me behind my back? Was I a strong man?

Ever since I'd been a kid, I was the one always asked for a euro in the metro, the kid chosen to carry little old ladies' shopping bags, help blind people across the street. I was the kid who was harassed or swindled by Jehovah's Witnesses, Seventh-Day Adventists, and UNICEF people when they came door-to-door. I had hoped that my good-guy face would fade with time, but it had stayed with me. My voice, thin for a man, and my body, emaciated by my forties, didn't help. No, people didn't see me as a strong man when they met me. Weak men get no respect.

I thought of my brother and how he operated. You can't make up success. It's forged when you're a kid. In a notebook that our mother bought him when he was a child, my brother had listed his wishes in order of priority: money, houses, women. Now, at the age of thirty-seven, he had two luxury apartments, one ex-wife, one wife, and a mistress.

When she came back into the room to wrap herself around my body, Zona was dressed in red, Shango red. In her arms, as solid as those of Cyclops, I felt like I was on the verge of returning to dust. She loosened her embrace, and in a theatrical voice that made me think there were more than just the three of us in the house, she announced that she had been charged with relaying a message to me. Then she sprinkled more drops of alcohol on the floor and lit incense that reeked of hay.

As I watched the gray smoke rise to the ceiling in columns, I thought, "What a drama queen, this Zona.". How many pounds of plants and fifths of rum did she waste each month to impress her patients?

Now she was talking in tongues, spitting like a fountain, grabbing me to shriek in my ear, "You have too much unhappiness inside you. You need to make peace with your father."

A moment later, I was outside, walking. The light was raw. Houses crammed together. Some Germans rolled past on Segways. A girl with green hair rode past on her bicycle. I crossed to the other sidewalk. Palm trees, more houses, more tourists, a Black man was busy digging a hole, my phone was vibrating, my legs trembling, my eyes filled with tears and this burning-hot day.

I cried, thinking about my father, about that morning I'd gone looking for him to talk man-to-man. A story I'd never told anyone. That Saturday morning, yes, when I'd gone back to Cameroon. I didn't yet do useless work at the bank, I didn't yet look like my mother, I looked like a young intern in a communications agency that was hiring, and I had the shoes to prove it.

I wasn't shown into the house immediately. First, I was led to a veranda. Never in my adult life, even if I was still only a boy at that point, had I felt such awkwardness about being no greater than myself, such fear about not being equal to this.

The barely pubescent maid brought me a soda and a roll of toilet paper for me to mop myself off—I was sweating bullets—and I questioned her like a tourist. She gave me her cell phone number, just in case, in case I was looking for a woman. I drank too quickly right out of the bottle, staining my shirt, of course, and Lovely the maid offered to clean it for me.

It was during this scene of ordinary Cameroonian life, with *the little maid sitting on the stranger's lap*, that my father appeared, paunchy as ever. Intact. Same massive size, same threat—two eyes in the forest—same beard, and same neck covered with hairs despite the time he spent plucking them, same brand-name shirt with turned-up collar.

He greeted me like men do there, foreheads bump, hands meet in a virile grip. He inflicted this greeting on me twice before turning to badger the maid: "Who stole my batteries? Who's been dipping into the coffee?" When my eyes dared move, they dropped to his shoes, a pair of sophisticated moccasins that betrayed the drama of a man who had conquered poverty by hurling it to the ground and trampling it. "You take a nap here, and they empty your coffee." He regularly marked and verified the level of coffee in the packets, alcohol in the bottles, and kept a record of the exact number of pieces of meat before storing them in the refrigerator. No question that he had become the boss. Our departure eleven years earlier had been good for him.

"You're that old?" he exclaimed when he learned my age. We made no reference to the past. My father lived in a modern world. What happened after that, what brought me to tears when I thought back to it, was so pathetic. His backside and jacket alone took up more than two-thirds of the bench. He dumped a trio of cell phones on the coffee table. He used them for business and the various mistresses he managed. Later, introducing me to one of them, he was brief. "This is Nathan. Say hello and see him to the door."

My morale had hit bottom, my shirt was dripping with sweat, so I dried out in the rental car, driving haphazardly around Yaoundé in the night. I didn't recognize the city of my childhood. Far from the main roads and street signs, I ended up losing my way in a neighborhood full of thieves and unfortunates, where guys on motorcycles descended on me, their faces hidden behind bandanas and ski caps. An instant later, I found myself barefoot, in my boxers, and stripped of my hairstyle, dubbed your-little-moron-hairstyle by the motorcycle thieves. I'd imported it from Paris for my return to Cameroon and the father who hadn't even looked at me.

In the city center where I made my way, I managed to lay my hands on a warm-up suit and some shoes. An itinerant barber worked on my head: "It's hard in this country. When my old man died, my stepmother went through his papers and stole everything. I tell you, life!

Two days later, I took the plane back to Paris without another visit to see my father, who had called in sick the day after our reunion. I wasn't after his money or his meat or his coffee. I had come to reclaim my name. I had come as a son.

Standing in front of the house, where I'd pounded on the front door with both fists, I swore to forget everything that had happened.

In the toilets at the coffee shop, I splashed a little water on my temples, keeping my head down to avoid looking at myself in the mirror. What Zona had *seen*, as she wrapped me in her arms, this supposed sorrow that she thought she was reading on my face, was no big deal. I no longer had a father, I could do nothing about it, but it wasn't the end of the world. I chased the priestess's words away by clapping my hands, the way you do to ward off evil, and had a fleeting vision—no doubt a devil's trick—of my body rotting away in a swamp, at least, a body that belonged to me. I recognized the forehead, the grimace, and the skin. I rushed back up to the main room of the coffee house, only young people there, with light, fresh hearts. Old people didn't last long in Bywater. They passed their mansion down to their beneficiaries and died in seaside villas in Florida or California. I soaked in the brouhaha of the living: people eating, people talking, people like the tall Black man with chestnut skin sitting behind me, complaining about the ill-deeds of modernity. This man of mixed race had grown up in New York and just bought a cottage in Faubourg Marigny, another neighborhood two blocks away. But in that neighborhood, he said, clasping his manicured hands together, everything was being disfigured. Gentrification was rising faster than the waters.

* * *

Small world. I saw the New Yorker again two days later at the big bourgeois ball where I presented myself, against my will, on my landlady's arm. On short notice, Denim had solicited me to replace the bastard who was supposed to accompany her. Marcus was the swine's name. The two of them were *amis améliorés*. English-speakers say *sex friends* or *friends with benefits*. We were in her limousine on our way to the Hyatt Regency where the event was taking place, as she described the bastard and briefed me on her love life. Denim was a woman alone. Her loneliness weighed more on her than her bank account.

An elevator dumped us out on the edge of the ballroom. A waiter seated us at a round table where eleven bourgeois notables were exchanging flatteries. There was the guy who had bought the cottage in Marigny, another one who had left L.A. to finish his novel, a woman who laughed like a brass band, a guy you thought you'd seen somewhere, a woman corporate lawyer who was retired, another woman insisting to her neighbor that when you grew older, you couldn't care less about wearing high heels, a man pissing himself at the idea of running into his mistress, a reformed politician who had converted to stand-up comedy, a young woman with a stain on her dress, another one who looked outdated, and the much-talked-about Angeleta, whose hairdo, a braided beehive about eight inches high and a foot wide, blocked my view of Astorga about whom she and Denim were talking again. In addition, around the boatload of tables laid with the same tablecloth, same dishes, was an assortment of mustaches, double chins, thick necks, authentic white teeth, power neckties, sorry plunging necklines, cross necklaces, hands in pockets, shop-keeper vests, shaved armpits, too-wide pants legs, *hello babies*, wandering eyes, unflattering dresses, suits pulled out of garment bags, and everywhere: the clatter of spoons-knives-forks layered on the music, the drone of the AC, and the voice of Zona, decked out in the same red dress that she'd worn at her house the other morning. She was hosting the event, she wouldn't let go of the microphone. The band persevered, but ambiance wasn't of primary importance. Above all, the bourgeois were there for the show, to distribute their business cards en masse, and to note phantom appointments on their electronic calendars. Style over substance.

I felt a presence behind me and recognized the man with the barrel chest and chicken legs I'd met at Denim's house the day after arriving in Louisiana. He was wearing a jacket with epaulettes that made him look even shorter. The sleeves broke at his wrists and his hands were fiddling with a pencil stamped with a fleur-de-lys, the emblem of this region, which had been French before Napoleon sold it off. The gnome leaned over to Denim who gave him the car keys, then he disappeared behind the waiter who was bringing drinks.

The table was drinking wine. The woman who only ran around in orthopedic shoes, was now declaring, "I benefit from both sides of life, wine and the Lord!" She sang at the St. Augustine Church every Sunday. Coincidentally, the man who had lived in L.A. was going to have his detective novel open in a church. He was a better liar than writer. From the way he responded to questions, I was pretty sure that he hadn't written a word and was counting on this kind of society event to make contact with an agent, an alchemist able to turn lead into gold. Remembering that I lived in Paris, he slipped me his business card and told me about his plans for the next five years.

I didn't have to protect my people, since the kook moved on to another spot. He sat down close to the student in a busty dress and was describing the bedroom furnishings and explaining why he never worked on Friday in a tone that encouraged her to read between the lines.

Aimlessly, I mixed with the people dancing, following their steps *pro forma*. At the other end of the dance floor, Angeleta was swaying like a pendulum with her three-layer-cake hairdo and her backside packaged in satin. The mixed-race guy and the woman lawyer were keeping her company. That's the most you could say, since the only part of their bodies moving was their mouth. I came across Ms. Sanctimonious again, who, under the effect of long sips of alcohol, was jerking a fast Charleston in circles around me. Her dress swelled with the movement. A balloon ready to pop. I was just about to sit down again when the beguine grabbed me by the waist. "Come on! Come on!" Just like Zaac had shouted the night we'd gone to hang out, when he'd taken me out to cut my teeth on the town, as they said. I pried myself from her grip and slid onto a seat at the table where I downed my glass of wine. I'd lost my appetite.

Like an automaton, I followed the arrow to the toilets and found myself two floors down in a dimly lit hallway. I hugged the walls, clenched my fists, and stamped my feet so I could feel my presence. If the floor under my feet, flickering neon, muffled sounds, and hum of the air conditioning were all real, that meant I also existed and the vertigo that had seized me a moment before, as I crossed the ballroom was normal, just a simple case of excess alcohol. Squatting down against the wall, I let my mind wander. I could see myself fighting my way through a forest. Not one of the safe, friendly forests you find in France, but a stingy forest, where the few trees I encountered offered no shade or cool relief. I got caught in prickly blackberry bushes, stepped over frayed tree roots, fallen trees sunk in the mud. When I came to a footbridge, just a narrow board stretched across a lake, and all the way at the bottom of the brackish waters, I could make out my own body, gangrenous with moss and quack grass. Somebody called my name, then I heard dogs and horses. Men were running after me. I could see them looming larger, red, like flames.

I don't believe in prophetic dreams. Still, when I opened my eyes, my heart was crashing like cymbals, as if this forest, sealed up like a coffin, surrounded me for real, as if I already knew that sometime soon I'd find myself there, alone and vulnerable. The light flicked on and I was shivering before the small-bodied man's for-real face, up close to mine. Denim had sent him down to look for me. She and Angeleta had left the ball and were waiting in the limousine. I stood up, still dizzy, and with all the strength I could muster, made my way to end of the corridor, descended the carpeted steps one by one. The elevators in the Hyatt were all occupied.

The short man with a small body took the lead, even though his legs were half as long as mine and despite the car accident that left him hard as a brick, and with a limp for life. He'd lost a lung and half his liver, Zaac said. But Zaac talks too much.

We had just reached the street when a swarm of horseback riders emerged at a gallop. We halted to let them pass. They were shouting "giddyap," and the mounts shot past in perfect formation. We stood there like two kids, admiring them. Then we headed straight for Denim's limousine. The gnome held the back door open for me, then turned the ignition, making the engine roar.

My landlady was sitting at an angle. One leg wrapped octopus-style around the other, she was replaying her most recent gambling adventures to herself, how and why she could have lost fifteen thousand dollars. She'd had two kings, which was great, but only two kings, when the player across the table had laid down his hand. Her joy had taken a nosedive because he had three of a kind. Consequently, she'd felt powerless and bet more than she'd planned to. That day, she was a woman who'd been taken down, and for her the blow had been even more terrible. She was used to winning. That was her weakness. When she played, she never thought about gambling just to gamble, she always thought about the other players. Which made her nervous, she felt it in her stomach, it went to her stomach every time someone was in the lead.

Before continuing, she swallowed hard, looked me straight in the eye. "I was too sure of myself when I walked into that room. I still had the taste of victory in my mouth. I was thinking of what I'd already won, not what I would get next. I forgot that there's also an element of luck. I wasn't focused enough. You know, when you get ready to do something, if you're thinking about what just happened, it's over. You've lost the game." Her hands dropped to her lap, her head rolled against the back of the seat. I contemplated her throat laden with strings of pearls, and her stiff, worn eyelids.

On the other seat, Angeleta had removed her wig and her hardware to drink champagne right out of the bottle. Her hands gripped the neck of the bottle of Chandon on which someone had written *The party starts here.* It was so cynical. In this luxury vehicle, which a servile chauffeur, up front behind the window, was guiding over the bumpy road, nothing signaled a party or the beginning of anything. It felt more like the end and rumination. Bent over her cell phone, Denim sighed over her most expensive poker game ever. She checked her precious stones, the poker chips, and the alligator-skin attaché case that held everything tightly in place. "Seven million, five hundred thousand dollars!" she cried, shoving the screen in Angeleta's face, Angeleta whose eyes were stubbornly turned toward the lights out the window, searching for Astorga.

The limousine turned onto an avenue of mansions with columns. I studied the terraces and the vast gardens. This was not the same city I'd seen, the one Zaac had shown me. No city bus came through here, no large families dangled plastic grocery bags. Nobody here tossed pebbles at boats out of boredom. Every resident had a car, good credit, a dog, children in the best schools, Colorado ski vacations or spa weeks in Santa Fe. Nobody had yet thought about taking down the Christmas lights. Spring was already here, but no hurry. The breeze was rocking the garden swings.

Angeleta inflicted one last guzzle of alcohol on her system and left the empty bottle to roll around under the seat. From the depths of the loneliness where she had sunk, everything seemed clearer. "He fucks all of them." Astorga had cheated on all of them, there was no longer any reason to get angry.

In the soothing quiet of the limousine, I thought about my sex life with the calm of a gynecologist for men. I took it easy with Jeanne, and we barely started before I wanted it to end. Screw, screw, screw the way Astorga screwed, I couldn't do it anymore. Even flirting had worn me out the other night, when the White woman from the women's bar hung all over me and swayed her flouncy hips at me.

I patted my hair into shape. Fatigue had cost my cheeks some of their shape, and I had new circles under my eyes. My two-tone three-piece and my afro that was too droopy to be stylish made me look like a serious man with no illusions.

Roughly speaking, the route past the plantations has only two landscapes. First, sugarcane, rising like spears for what seems like a hundred miles to Baton Rouge. Then cotton, masses of shriveled bushes that looked insignificant from the road. Beyond the fields, dust: automobile carcasses, skeletal trees, strip malls, bayous, gas stations, road signs presuming future lanes, store signs, and a small sign announcing that we would soon be there. In under twenty miles, we'd arrive at Evergreen Plantation, where "the phone book" worked, the woman who knew everything, and where, for all I knew, my uncle had washed ashore.

Zaac navigated the pick-up truck humming a little roulée. Engrossed in the immensity of the sky that pressed down on us, he'd stopped talking, stopped smoking. We had set off at dawn and stopped at a diner for breakfast: coffee for me, and for him, a French vanilla to which he'd added six fingers of a Mezcal Añejo from a cowhide flask. Which hadn't prevented him from thinking things through or making proposals. First off, he reminded me that money was not an issue. He was offering me his expertise; I would only dig into my pocket for gas and drinks. His time was also a gift. We'd take our whole lifetime, if necessary, to find out what had happened to the great uncle. "Family is sacred." I merely nodded because I felt all tight inside. Sacred. That meant it couldn't be touched. Relations with my people would stay as they were, tense and conflicted.

For years I had refused to acknowledge this, instead foisting my troubles onto France. I thought it was because of France that I'd become a chewed-up man, a Negro-towel-head-wop with no spine and no homeland under my feet. For two years I'd bored a shrink with my immigrant melodrama until I admitted that France, my cannibal, was not to blame. It was a family thing for us, to figure out among us.

I have already talked about my failed return to Yaoundé when I was twenty, and the fiasco at my father's house. I got just as mired with my mother who defended herself by insisting that she'd done her best. She had torn me from Cameroon for reasons that should not be questioned. Without her, I would have ended up a drunk or an imbecile like *that other one.*

I studied the Louisiana sky, and it looked pale to me. Above the sun now reduced to a single ray, the clouds were accumulating like packets of sadness, sheep with no shepherd, at the mercy of the wolf. I looked at the too-vast sky hanging above this earth that was insufficient. The sky was famished. I felt its maw weighing down the roof of the pick-up-truck cabin. I smelled its breath in the bed of the truck. The air was heavy, and I was having trouble breathing.

Eyes glued to the road, his flask two-thirds empty and within reach, Zaac also seemed to be inside his head. I had no idea what he was brooding about. Maybe a woman or maybe his mother who lived in Arabi and made gumbo like nobody else. She'd had Zaac with a man who'd died too soon, and who continued to talk to her in her dreams. She said that he told her they were so much better off and happier *up there*. Zaac's mother believed in Heaven. Her life was gumbo and church, that's it.

Before the plantation, we stopped at a gas station, and I walked over to some houses grouped next to a cotton field. I'd never seen a cotton plant up close. The old films didn't show the picking in detail, the cut palms, the bleeding fingers, the puss oozing out around the fingernails. I unfastened a boll and squeezed it in the hollow of my hand. It was light, felt weightless, and yet, these little pompoms had built the South and the glory of the masters. This was what the masters dreamed about as they dozed in the evening on their shaded verandas, safe and peaceful, safe and peaceful.

Cotton is the father of all. Cotton is the mother of everyone. Cotton to clothe us, to feed us, enrich us. Cotton made the South. Cotton is the South. Cotton is good for the South and the South is good for cotton. Germany, England, France, Italy, Spain are hungry for cotton. Only the hand can separate the seed from the leaf. More arms mean more cotton. More cotton means more money. Cotton is the father and the mother of the Old South. Hail to Cotton, you who made us rich and powerful. A salute to you who reign over the South and keep us from misery and calamity. Good health and long life to you, the All-Powerful.

Safe. But not so peaceful since they knew that nothing would last. One insane fire, one thrashing by the sky, one pitifully small harvest and the king would die. A few leagues from the cabins, beyond the paved path bordered by mossy trees, you could imagine the worried silhouettes. Eyes never closed, sleep never deep, their rifles at the ready. How could they be at peace, not fear the men-made-beasts, whose females suckled their own infants? Knowing, as sure as a knife could slit a throat, that one morning those devilish beasts would scale the steps to their house, four at a time, kick in their bedroom door, burn their balls, and make off with their women?

The worst was not knowing when.

I went back to the truck, where Zaac was opening a beer. "You know what? Today, I'm going to play God. I'm the only one who pays." He pointed to the six-packs tossed onto the back seat and the wad of bills peeking out of his pocket to impress Amber, the half-and-half Latino-plus-Black woman who had fled from his life right when he lost his job as assistant stockboy at the big Whole Foods store for the swanky folk on Magazine Street. She left me that very day, he said. Not a day later, but that very day. "And you know what? I chased after her like a dog." I ran the scene through my mind, trying to picture Zaac's ex. Probably proud of her light skin and hair that hung down to her behind. No doubt you saw her coming from a distance, turning heads as she walked by—"You look so good, baby"—while her perfect shape swiveling under a skimpy skirt or shorts, and this is where you missed something, indicated that she was not free but had a steady, so don't touch. I also imagined her hurry to get hitched long-term with Zaac, her starry-eyed excitement for Zaac, the bad boy, and then her complete U-turn a year later: her discouragement, her inconsideration for this angry man incapable of holding down a job.

* * *

We had arrived. Behind the picture-perfect gate of the plantation, two rows of oak trees stretched to infinity. Slouching toward one another like a column of hunchbacked ogres, the trees filtered out all but golden light from the sky. Beneath the gleaming, entangled branches, the central path glowed as if paved with Louis d'or. Seemed like it should lead to a palace.

In the parking lot, currently shared by a dozen vehicles, Zaac was still elaborating his story. After being fired, he'd gone home and just put *his feet under the table*, as women leap to say when a man sits down at the table, not even asking what's for dinner. But he hadn't sat down in the kitchen for his stomach. That night, he needed to talk. "A woman should be there for that, too, right?"

On that point we agreed. I listened to him describe the end of the evening. All Zaac's evenings came to a bad end: an argument, a man hurt, a woman crying, regrets, bitterness, and padding with alcohol to forget.

He patted his overstuffed jacket pocket triumphantly. Amber? She'd soon be eating out of his hand. He would offer her what that loser Evan, who was circling in on her, didn't have the means to offer her. Amber liked to dance, so he'd take her dancing. She liked to chow down, he'd take her to a seafood restaurant where they emphasized the attractive presentation over the number of critters on the plate. Amber was his, and she would stay his, despite the slights that she had dumped on him the other night, saying she was done with having a gypsy in her bed, she was a woman of higher quality and deserved, for this reason, higher-quality treatment. "What could I say to that? What would you have done in my shoes?" I had no idea. He hadn't pressed the matter, afraid she might lift her dreamy fanny off the chair and call the police to lodge a domestic violence complaint.

Zaac extracted two pairs of plastic boots from the trunk. The ground around here soaked into your bones. It acted like it was the sky. Sometimes it seemed like it was raining under your feet. I pulled the boots on and followed Zaac, taking small steps, listening to the squelch of rubber shoving its way into the sediment.

I had spent part of my childhood playing in the mud with friends. When the great rains fell, we made a dash for the biggest holes in the neighborhood, wanting to be the first to jump in. We jumped in fully dressed, splashed around, and fought. But it was afterwards that we took the real blows, when our mothers, their backs aching from scrubbing our clothes, gave us a good hiding.

The tour had already begun when I joined the group of tourists who were strolling up the wide, tree-lined path. I'd fallen behind at the cash register because Zaac refused to pay the entry fee. Calling the employees vultures, he walked out. I paid my thirty dollars anyway to see the mansion up close. After the ninety-minute visit, I'd go back and find Zaac. We'd go talk to Lewis, the woman who knew more than a phone book, who knew the region and the history of the farm workers. The big house was pictured in the brochure that came with the entry ticket, as well as two bachelor apartments, twenty-two slave cabins, a vegetable garden, two dovecotes, a cottage, some sugarcane fields, cotton fields, and a lake.

The guide was beginning the chapter on the lake when I joined the group. With his Jimmy Carter smile and bushy eyebrows that met in the middle, Edgar Heiner explained why this lake was called Lac des Allemands. After the Indian massacre, they had to find farmers to feed the town and run the plantation. So, they went off to find some Germans.

Then he cracked a joke about the German temperament and their well-known penchant for sausage. He was well-positioned to talk about it since his own ancestors had come over to America on a boat from Hamburg. In North Carolina, where they had first put down roots, they'd opened an upscale grocery called Wurst-Heiner. Heiner, like his last name. Wurst, like the German word for "sausage."

Faces softened. That was probably what made a guide good: an ability to put you at ease and to sell you something nice to overlay the sordidness while discreetly consulting his watch to avoid running overtime.

As we continued the tour, Heiner pointed out a tight row of willow trees like a fence around a vegetable garden. "Willows are the first to leaf out in the spring. In winter, when the wind blows, you can hear their leaves falling. They fall all night and make so much noise that it sounds like rain." Certain cypresses also lost their robe. Because some of the branches were covered with Spanish moss, they were said to be bald, bald and bearded. Two of them were leaning forward as if the wind had pushed them, either to break them in half or force them to their knees. Did they remember the song of King Cotton? Did they feel sorrow or hostility when they recalled scenes of daily life when white adults and children, all worked up, shouted "Kill him!" to the one who was going to die anyway? "Kill him!" to those they tortured methodically and assiduously? Was it leaves or tears that flowed from these trees that had witnessed crowds burning and hanging men?

At the end of the long vault of trees stood the residence, known for its horseshoe staircase, but especially for the scenes from *Django Unchained* filmed here, as well as the *Roots* series remake. We all took pictures of the facade, everyone, the same photo, then Heiner pointed out the marble in the columns and on the blue ceiling of the entry porch. "In Africa, they put blue there to keep the spirits from entering the habitations." His eyes searched for mine.

Inside the house, the rooms were not terribly large and the furnishings, sparse. The heads of those who had lived there hung on the walls in abundance. The saga of the Becnels, the principal occupants, went on forever. Heiner told us who'd slept with whom, who'd made a bastard with whom, who'd been crazy, cruel, nice, rich, or crippled by debt.

I stepped out onto the upper balcony where, in the film, DiCaprio's sister almost swoons upon seeing Django, dressed in a suit and armed with a pistol, emerge on horseback. From here, Heiner's fables seemed even more unnecessary. His jokes hit like curses.

I walked out to the cabins alone. For close to a century, this was where the slaves had reproduced among themselves. The habitations, that no fire, hurricane, or war had managed to demolish, dated from 1800. Hardly credible, given what they were made of: old wood, red brick, and sheet metal for the roof.

A sign at the entrance to the quarters detailed the chores. The slaves didn't just pick cotton, their sweat ran twenty-four hours a day. The Lord hadn't given them a single day off.

In one of the cabins open to the public, I was surprised to find a chair and a wooden bed frame. Yet Heiner had sworn that the cabins were of the period. And the descendants of the ones at peace, the sons of the sons of the masters, sighed, absolved. They had not come here to hear about slavery.

I saw them arrive at a trot behind Heiner, walk past the cabins without entering them, and listen with a credulous ear to his fantastic recitation of the life of the "workers."

At Evergreen, Heiner said without blinking, Sunday was not a day of work. The Blacks played the banjo, cultivated their garden patch, and went to church. The proof was this chapel without a roof, a simple garden, like the ones that existed at the time, with a rustic cross with no Jesus, and pine benches with no slaves.

The tour ended. The group made its way to the restrooms and gift shop. Zaac wasn't wrong: they had cheated us then and were cheating us still. Hell was still hell. Truth doesn't grow back as hell.

"Did you enjoy the tour?" I turned around to look at Heiner, who was still standing on the steps of the cabin, his smile gone, a thermos in his hand. This was his break. It was his break, and he was taking advantage of it to remember Charlotte, the city where he'd grown up in the days when you only spoke to a Black person to give them an order or a kick in the pants. Great-grandson of immigrants that he was, he'd grown up in the skin of a White accustomed to shouting, "Do it again," "Get out of here," "Come here," expecting to have the door held open for him, expecting them to lower their eyes in his presence, take off their hat to speak to him. Heiner had been a White and could do nothing about it. "This will end when we're all the same race. In the end, we will all have to be the same color."

I said nothing and watched him stroke his mustache. His intentions were good, but his narrowed eyes looking like buttons on shirt cuffs hinted at his unease. He felt awkward having to engage in this conversation so early in the morning.

It came both too early and too late. At the age of sixty, he'd seen the world go in both directions. He'd seen it move forward and backwards.

"Don't believe everything you see in films. In the past, it wasn't because we were mean that we didn't speak to our maid. It just wasn't done. We grew up with the Jim Crow laws, and that's the way it was. For a long time. Now that it's over, there are Blacks who want to put up barriers. They say we still have our old mentality. But me, at least, I don't have any prejudices. Habits, yes, but not prejudices."

He cleared his throat to say goodbye and I felt his heart beat in my palm. Half a life it had taken for that gesture not to bother him, shaking the hand of a Black man. It would never be a habit.

He couldn't bring himself to leave. "So, tell me, how are houses built where you're from?"

I left Yaoundé when I was twelve years old. I don't know what the houses are like or the roads, or the trees, or the inhabitants. I fled with my mother because I was small enough to fit in the trunk of a car. I didn't see the road between Yaoundé and Douala. I wasn't scared. My mother was resistant, a wildflower that never bloomed in a vase. So she kept going, despite the stream of trucks, the cracked asphalt, and the heat of that vile March. When the city appeared, she pulled me out of my hiding place and dusted off my clothes. I didn't ask questions. In Paris, we lived in a hostel until Mathieu was born, then we moved into an apartment that was smaller than the Becnel big-house upper balcony.

I stared into Heiner's gray eyes and saw nothing in them but fatigue. We'd gotten nowhere this morning, the two of us. The barriers were holding strong. The routine was starting over. A new bus of visitors had just pulled into the parking lot.

***

When you looked at Lewis, you didn't see a woman, you saw a shape with uncertain contours, diluted in an office probably containing as many archives as the Williams Research Center on Chartres Street, where I had wasted two days examining microfiches and killed three viewing machines. Lewis, born in a redneck shantytown, had ended up becoming a better person by landing the title of Ma'am Evergreen. They said she was married to the plantation. She had dropped anchor there forty-seven years before and used this excuse not to marry. In her world, men didn't exist. Machines, either. She calculated in her head and wrote by hand. In notebooks with little squares that she ordered from France, she noted down everything that had happened at Evergreen. Not only the tribulations of Becnel and his relatives, but also all the stories that came after, like the one about Blacks who had made a commitment to keep cultivating the earth after the South had been demolished and the end of slavery proclaimed.

This same Lewis was now in her chair, doubled over with laughter as Zaac told her the difference between a hotdog-eating-contest competitor from Alabama and a shrimp gorger from Louisiana. She repeated the riddle, mopping her beady eyes, so riotous was it. The two laughed so well together.

For that was also the South. A world where you kissed your enemy on the mouth. Where, beyond the fear that would continue to inspire them mutually and eternally, Blacks and Whites were still brothers. Blacks and Whites alike understood that a White baby nourished by a Black woman's milk and fluids is no longer totally white. And a Black person who cleans up White people's shit is no longer totally black.

I thought back to the bus stop, to those Blacks who were close to falling, those left to fall, and held back my tears. Nothing would happen in this shiny, modern America that we'd been sold, for those audacious enough to be free. I especially had bought into it. We might shout that it should all be burned down, but who would strike the match? There would be no revolution.

In a letter, Etienne John Wayne Marie-Pierre announced his arrival. After weeks at sea, he could see land from his cargo ship. New Orleans was a seductive woman, but he made his way directly to Baton Rouge. Because that's where the money and the fields were. He hadn't left Douala to twiddle his thumbs. Another letter, from what I understood, also made it back across the waters, a postcard picturing a landscape that could have been anywhere. That's the last time Etienne John Wayne Marie-Pierre wrote home. After 1956, everything had to be imagined.

Becoming American wasn't in our family genes. German? Maybe. French, we already were, in a way. But America was different. On the evenings we had electricity, we started dreaming about it at the cinema.

I focused on the sound of Lewis's pencil scratching on the paper. It was the same pencil that Denim used on her rental contracts. A way to show that what was written could be changed, that her word was just as valid.

A clerk told Lewis that a worker had been injured in an accident the previous evening. More fright than harm. Two fingers gone. Lewis lifted herself from her seat and trailed to the door where the mutilated worker was standing. He was a dark-haired man, about twenty years old with a voice that made him sound puny, and forearms that had been reduced to tools by the brutish shovel, the cumbersome machete, and the soil, the soil. Lewis unrolled two twenty-dollar bills and laid them on the part of his hand that remained. Then she shut the door, furrowing her brow like you do when you've suddenly remembered something. Almost nothing. She didn't want me to lose my head.

When I turned toward her, she had disappeared behind an armoire. She had climbed up onto a stepladder and was feeling around for something on top of the cornice. I could hear her shifting objects. She came down with a shoebox patched with scotch tape. "These are old things that the guys have left behind." She tried to decipher the reference written on the box. "Apparently, this one dates from when your old man was here. If he was here."

Suddenly, a bang. I thought someone was kicking down the door, but it was Zaac, happy for me, and so pleased to have brought me here that he'd knocked his chair over. Now, that's something to celebrate, we'll have to drink to that for sure, he exclaimed, dialing the number of Jeri, his friend, dearer to him than a sister, and who lived nearby.

I took the box, and certified to Lewis that I would plead guilty if I lost or damaged its contents. Everything was listed on the form to be signed, but the American insisted on going over the rules with me. She spoke directly, like a sheriff, with no hint of courtesy in her rodent eyes. Her demeanor improved when I showed my identity card. I was a real Frenchman and that counted for something.

On the way to see Jeri, I wondered what I was going to do with all this. Not so much with the shoebox, presiding at my feet like a divinity, but the rest: Jeanne's charity and my mother's bitterness. I would not cut myself off from them. Soon my mother would call to ask me for an update and compare me to my brother. She never used his name when quoting him, it was always "your brother," the way you say "God," "taxes" or "the President." Your brother, she'd repeat, for she might use the expression ten times in the same sentence. Then she'd remind me, as if I could forget, how much ambition and merit her younger son showed. Jeanne had invited them over for dinner at the apartment in the 12th arrondissement. Those three would soon get along like ravens from the same nest.

Jeri was entering her early forties with a son in high school whom she was raising all on her own, a sick aunt, an alcoholic mother, an activist uncle, and two doctorates. After law school, she had steeped herself in political science, anthropology, and Haitian literature. She could stumble along in French. She had gone to Haiti once. She told me all that while savoring fried catfish filets and hitching up the straps of her dress that fell in soft folds over her stomach.

I wasn't sure if she had nice legs. As long as women have their shoes on, their legs are a mystery. Not sure either if I understood where she was going with this, why her mouth, in movement to that point, had suddenly tightened and targeted me like a question mark.

Jeri wasn't waiting for anything specific. As quickly as she'd stopped talking, she picked up her monologue again, eyeing her square of rice and the last filet. "Vacation came, and our parents sent us to summer camps for militants. They were like intellectual reeducation camps where they taught us a history not taught in white schools. One day, we had to draw slave ships and the leader showed us on a map where they had sailed. That was a lot of boats and slaves by the end of the summer."

This time, she just let her straps slip down and wiped her forehead with a paper tissue. There was nothing you could do in the face of a broken-down air conditioner. It was always the same story at this diner, but no one complained. As if this awful heat added flavor to the catfish, and that absent these conditions—the box of tissues on the table, our sweat dribbling onto the plates, the ceiling fans lurching, the "God, it's hot!"—the catfish would be reduced to just any old boneless fish.

Jeri downed a glass of ice water and pushed her empty plate aside. She had eaten everything to avoid wasting food, but the fish here was too heavy, not surprising when you saw the cook, too greasy, too salty, that's not cooking.

She asked me if I liked to cook, what my uncle had been like, what I liked to read, if I'd had time to go fishing, or do a little tourism. She asked questions in bulk, take them or leave them. Her intelligence appealed to me.

"Zaac thinks we should boycott the plantations."

"In that case, we'd have to boycott the entire South," she said. "We'd have to burn all the bad flags still flying and decapitate the statues."

She changed the subject when Zaac came back from the restroom, his fly only half-zipped and his shirt dripping wet; he had vomited on it. She confiscated the beer that he was about to finish off, surprised that a man like me could hang out with such a sketchy character.

You didn't run into Zaac, he picked you, and took you around in his pick-up truck when he was in the mood and had the time. You didn't leave him either, he disappeared. You thought he was behind you and turned around to talk to him, and surprise! The rascal had run off. Zaac lived in his world. It was a ghetto, but there he was king.

Jeri brought her eyes back to me, and I met her gaze, not understanding. There was nothing to understand. It was enough just to laugh and revel in this proof that we weren't alone on this night. The three of us were together and would remember this moment for a long time, even twenty years later, Zaac, Jeri, and I, each in our own place, with the same spirit, the emotion intact. It was a beautiful evening.

A beautiful evening in a place that wasn't worth a nickel, where it never would have occurred to me to stop with Jeanne. There were only locals here, and the place was black, absolutely black, from the waitress to the cook, from the cook to the girl with locks, from the girl with locks to her pander, her man, or maybe her brother. Zaac, who claimed to know everyone wherever he went, claimed to have run into him somewhere and called him Roger.

"I'm telling you, I'm not your man!" the guy retorted, gripping the skinny arm of the girl with long hair. But a gust of old songs flowing from the radio scattered his words.

Just as Zaac was about to lay into Roger, Jeri got up and grabbed him by the collar. She gave him a talking to like she would to a child, her fist clenched and ready, in case he didn't get his head on straight. She didn't need to use it. Zaac slumped onto the chair, whining.

"Next time, I'll punch him," she said, not because she wanted to impress me but because it would never happen. She and Zaac, and she had intoned this several times over dinner, they were like Monday and Tuesday, you didn't get one without the other. He'd been there for her, she'd been there for him, anytime anything went wrong.

She stood her rascal up on his feet, paid the check, and decided to have us stay the night at her house. She had recovered her American voice and stride. She moved toward the exit, almost at a run, making her legs less visible than ever.

* * *

There are houses that look like houses. They have shadows that take us back to childhood, to the shared space from an ideal time when we assume that we were happy and loved. Jeri's house had that effect on me. No fence, no security cameras, no alarms on the doors or windows. We went in and found a place to sit down while Jeri opened the living-room windows and set ice and a bottle out on the table. I accepted one last glass so my hands wouldn't be empty. I drank my beer, listening to the crickets. So perfect, it sounded like a record.

Near the club chair where I was sitting, Zaac was sleeping, wrapped in a sheet. It had taken two of us to pull off his boots and wedge him onto the sofa. He could sleep there, said Jeri, carrying my belongings into her son's bedroom. Alex was spending the night at a cousin's house. Jeri went off to take a shower and change her clothes.

Now my awareness of my surroundings was limited to her voice and the scent of soap. In the low, indirect light from the lamps, she was a form, moving to open the fridge, break open an ice cube tray, fill our glasses.

"We're afraid and that's why things don't change," she murmured. "We're afraid that we're not good people anymore, and that God is kicking us in the butt. But everybody's killing everybody. Killing children who are going to school, killing people in churches. Last year, right near here, we even had a grandmother kill her grandson. She pulled the trigger because she'd heard a noise."

The body from which her voice was coming continued to go about its business in the room. If you'd turned down the sound, it would have looked like Jeri was talking to me about art and literature. The depth of a person's pain can't be measured with the naked eye. But I knew that this friend of Zaac sometimes lost it, went into her son's room to warn him. You can do better, you must do better, because they're waiting for you at the foot of a tree with a rope and a can of gasoline. I imagined Alex's exasperated face. That didn't concern him, it was all in the past.

There was an old-fashioned record player in the living room, purchased for almost nothing at a garage sale, which only worked with certain kinds of music and certain albums. "He adores anything by Nina Simone," said Jeri, lifting the lid of the antique turntable where a 45-rpm record by the diva already lay waiting patiently. With maniacal delicacy, she set the machine in motion.

Simone started singing. Jeri gazed at the vinyl record, nodding. I wasn't sure if she was nodding her approval or starting to dance. I watched Jeri sway slightly, and in her body that held back from going further, hesitated to give itself over to it, I felt like I was seeing Nina Simone again, the day she asked her spectators what kind of men they were, were they ready to start a revolution? She had howled the question. Yet, it wasn't the end of the Black people of America. They still had two more capable Christs, two living heroes who would be assassinated a short time later.

Jeri knew this story and others. Her father's brother had an affair with the singer. You might call it love. You should call it love. Both had served the cause.

Jeri lowered the volume and lit a cigarette.

"Your wife, is she French?"

With Zaac, I had talked about my romantic situation without mentioning the fact that Jeanne was not black. A futile precaution. They probably sensed it as soon as they met me, and as I suspected, they considered it a problem.

Awkwardly, I corrected her, not sure what I should say or obscure. "We're not married." I watched the slow curls of smoke surround Jeri, aware that they were distancing her from me.

Suddenly, the ceiling lurched as if something had dropped onto the roof and was rolling across it. It was those damn raccoons, and the damn neighbor who kept putting dishes of food out in the yard to feed her nine cats. The police had decreed that it was her right when Jeri called them to come and take a look at the mess. There were now raccoons in the garbage cans, in the attics, all over the neighborhood, and even opossums. Didn't matter, the law is the law, and you can't forbid a citizen to feed her cats. You also can't kill your neighbor's cats. Jeri took a drag on her cigarette. Unless you did it quietly, after the neighbor had gone to work.

She'd poisoned two of them last month, there were seven left. What also helped was the pump-action shotgun. Not for the cats but for the racoons. But the gun was heavy, and the racoons were quick. So far, no success. It seemed like the more she loaded, the more commotion there was on the roof. She crushed out her cigarette and cracked her knuckles. "I'll see you in the morning, God willing."

She was lying. God had nothing to do with it. She was regretting having opened her house to a man who was almost married to a white woman. I stammered goodnight and a few other trite phrases to free her and remained in the armchair, which was nothing more than a reprieve, listening to the night, then hearing nothing.

Amid the roots of my childhood, I was moving forward, my heart fearful and my calves all scraped up. I had taken so many twists and turns. I was sinking in a crumbling city. I was walking up streets with no sidewalks. It was Yaoundé but not

Yaoundé, and the backpack I was carrying was so heavy. I should have traveled light. I recognized the cursed forest of the other night. Sometimes dreams seem to lie in wait. I was on that same pedestrian bridge, I was seeing the putrid waters again, and my ghost. I sat down.

The commotion started up again but sounded different. As if the rodents, crashing down off the roof, were now outside the front door, trying to force it open. I examined the door. It was made of cypress, just like the columns, hardwood floor, table, corner hutch, cutting board, and crate with twelve holes for Jeri's returnable bottles if she forgot to take them back. Safe, solid cypress, not like the toothpick trees I'd seen on Interstate 10 when Zaac's pick-up truck was shooting across the Lake Ponchartrain causeway at top speed.

Worried, I glanced out the window. Good Lord, Jeri wasn't kidding. Filthy beasts! They would squat in the houses if allowed, and it would take more than a shotgun to dislodge them. I shuddered with disgust and went back over to Zaac, who was now curled into the fetal position and snoring, his arms on top of the sheet. His watch said it was 4:13 a.m.

It was only later that I remembered the box. I opened it with the apprehension of disinterring a corpse. Then came the bitterness of realizing it wasn't the right one. Nothing in this cardboard box filled with rags and bits and pieces had belonged to Wayne. Lewis had the wrong story. After all, she was just an old goat with an old memory and a pile of notebooks filled with drivel. I was sorry to have come here to meet her. My eyes lingered on Zaac. Think what you want, but two sorry souls don't go together. It's bad luck for them to associate.

I went into Alex's room, laid the emptied box on the bed, and hung up my clothes. Tomorrow, I'd have to pursue another avenue and have a serious discussion with Zaac. I had one month left before my return to France.

As I was putting all this nonsense back into the box, I noticed a bundle of papers hidden under the strings, letters dating from almost two centuries before, and which Heiner the tour guide, merchant of nostalgia, could have put to good use. They were the work of a planter's wife, one of those Southern Belles that Zaac was sorry hadn't been hanged. He had such a comical way of being sorry that you couldn't help laughing. His voice rose to a high pitch, and minced around as if dressed in a crinoline gown, descending the stairs of a mansion.

I continued going through these archives, but there was so little of use, so little to read besides one or two passages about the slaves, that I dozed off, with the light still on, to the scent of clean sheets and anti-mosquito incense.

* * *

Jeri had already left when I got out of bed. Zaac was reheating the coffee and fulminating against Amber. It's true that it lacked grace to dump a man's belongings on the sidewalk, a man who had asked for your hand in marriage. It's also true that she had promised to do it if Zaac took exception to paying his share of the rent. That's what I was explaining to Zaac who was refusing to listen and accusing me of always being against him.

This is how it ended: we didn't even touch Jeri's coffee, we left with the box and got back on the I-10, listening to WWOZ, where trumpeter Christian Scott was talking about how he stretched his jazz by combining it with the music of his Native American grandparents. One of his most recent titles was *The Big Chief*. It paid homage to the beliefs of the ancestors. The host discussed it as if talking about an exceptional piece. To which Scott replied that it was mostly his grandfather who was exceptional. He had won his battle against America by refusing its dollars and its whiskey.

Jeri called Zaac back just as the pick-up truck was merging onto St. Bernard Avenue. I heard her full-throated laugh flowing out of the cell phone and was relieved that she didn't ask to speak to me. That's how it should be. Friendship should not be forced.

"Shit!" grumbled Zaac, turning back into the gas station parking lot located at the corner of Rampart and Governor Nicholls. It was impossible to go any further. An ambulance and three police cars were blocking the road. The neighbors, who had gathered on the pavement, were talking, but not like usual. Their voices were low and shaky, mouths and their whole bodies strained toward the victim on the stretcher.

A cop was questioning a vendor, a witness to the scene. "People shouldn't die so fast and so young." It wasn't an objective response, but it calmed things down a little. It gave the illusion of being able to fight against death. "There she was, playing in the street, then a minute later she didn't move anymore." Regardless of how the vendor tried to choose his words, what he was saying didn't make any sense. So, he added details. Janet had jumped into everyone's lap. That's all the little girl had ever done in life, jump into adults' laps. She hadn't had time to do anything bad.

The police officer seemed just as distraught. The death that he usually rubbed elbows with had a different face. It never distressed him when it occurred. He didn't hesitate to say "good riddance," always begging the Devil at the end of his day to give him the strength to confront the worst. Press him a little and you'd understand what he was talking about. The worst was when the community killed the community, when brothers of the same blood and the same milk tore each other to pieces like wild dogs, when a father violated his daughter, when a son brought shame to his mother, when instead of walking straight and together the same people declared war on one another and accused the system of creating this system. "We also have to question ourselves." That's as far as the officer went when they let him talk. Then he got back in his patrol car, fear gripping him between the thighs. The next one on the stretcher could be his son.

Another policeman raised his arm. The crowd submitted to the law. The ambulance, impotent as a hearse, started rolling. Turned toward the vehicle, Zaac was even stiffer than the little girl who was inexplicably dead. Behind him stood my neighbor, her companion Paul, as well an elderly woman I assumed to be Brenda, the famous sister of Janet's grand-mother, because she had green eyes and almost-white skin. The Creole woman, whose still-agile hands were twisting a pair of rollerblades, spoke to Zaac. She had been in the kitchen when Janet went out to play. She should have forbidden her to roller-skate outside, but these days they didn't go out in the yard because of the construction work and the hole for the swimming pool. Paul wrapped his arms around her and nodded mechanically to me. I responded, and I felt as though, by returning his greeting, I was returning his story to him, the story he had offered me that Sunday when I felt dizzy, my first Sunday in Tremé, the one about white people's past being so swollen with their skin color that some made a big fuss about it and blew their lid.

I thought back to Brenda, a young woman on that Pittsburgh morning when she had abandoned her infant on the steps of the church to palm him off on the good Lord. Paul had no idea how she'd felt, whether she'd had doubts, felt shame. Now that Janet was dead, I preferred to think that she'd felt both hesitation and abjection, and that she had bent down to inspect the child, full of hope, as if crossing the city so early in the morning, almost falling and almost being hit by a car might erase all this black on the little baby, might, with one swipe, make him less dark than a brown-paper bag. All the same, she'd still abandoned him.

And here she was, sixty years later, paying for the deed done, tearing at the skin on her chest, begging for forgiveness, forgive me, forgive me, forgive me Lord for the lamb sacrificed at dawn. If only he had struck her down immediately instead of waiting until this moment. And an innocent child, yet! Leaning on a neighbor's shoulder, she turned toward where the ambulance had driven off. They would let her trot after it for a few yards. The path to purgatory is never direct. Standing among the others, I heard her supplications echoed by those who had stayed on their doorstep. I listened to this choir born in pain and indignation. Was I also indignant? I wasn't sure but it seemed right to me, this voice coming from I-don't-know-which mouth, which face—we're all same in the eyes of death—and which said: you got a free meal this morning, hmm, Grim Reaper?

* * *

As I took out my garbage cans, I spied Mrs. Crouch on the sidewalk across the street. Mrs. Crouch was the Faulknerian Black Woman, a persevering figure who never complained about anything and embodied only a limited range of habits. At five o'clock every afternoon, she opened the front door of her shotgun bungalow, took a few steps out the door, stopped, and shifted her position only when the sun moved. We saw her drift toward it, hang out for a time, long enough to warm her bones, then go back into the house where she lived with her great-grandson, a well-meaning young boy who had just gotten out of jail. I observed her work shoes and her mismatched, handknit clothes. She had combined blue and chestnut brown. A New Orleans Saints ski cap topped her head. Of the body that had served everywhere, at the hospital, plantation, school, hotel, church, people's houses, houses of White folks, all you could see was a narrow strip of calf between the hem of her skirt and the top of her socks.

"Hello, Mrs. Crouch." I knew she wouldn't answer. She would wait until I had my head down or back turned before greeting me. There was nothing mean in that, it was just her way. She timed her hello with the moment I walked back into my yard, and I heard her taking a crazy amount of time to maneuver her legs out to the sidewalk. She wasn't made of sugar, but she'd had her share of years, and age only moves in one direction.

I turned on the two lamps in my bedroom, retreated to the sofa-bed, and did nothing else. The last sounds of the day reached me from the street. Darkness was coming but the night would not take over.

No young people smoking together out on the stoop or cosseting their car out front. No old people sitting out front, keeping an eye on the neighborhood. No stories with laughter. No lovers whistling because they have a date. No women locked in the bathroom to make themselves beautiful, or naked. On this night when not even a child was worth more than a speck of dust, they'd turn on the television and shut the front door. Behind the wall with the stove, the dish drain, and the refrigerator-freezer all squeezed together, I listened to Trump explain how to deal with the Mexicans. Lewis had given money to the farmworker who had ripped up his hand while forcing the ground open. Two twenty-dollar bills, enough to buy a few six-packs of beer, enough to see what was coming. What boss was going to want a cripple? What would America want with a one-armed migrant, even for free, even when the useless one was willing to sleep in the former slave quarters, miraculously intact, as the guide had said, and evidently still functioning, accommodating the most absolute poor? How many had suffered in them since the great dispersion? How many bodies had gotten up dead in the morning? How many Sosos, Mulattos, Congos, Creoles, American Negroes? How many trustworthy Negroes, sweet and docile, how many of the John-can-ride-horseback, Little-Geneviève-a-hard-worker, Gabriel-can-talk-to-animals, Achilles-with-crippled-legs, Joseph-with-bad-temperament?

All had been recorded in scrupulous detail, so that, in the case of the master's death, the inventory would be clearly outlined: three bed sets, two mattresses, five woolen blankets, a mosquito net, two bedsteads made of cypress, a lot of seventeen slaves, one coffee pot, two dozen forks of normal size, four draft horses, one soup tureen, one sugar bowl, three milk cans.

I pulled my head down into my neck, my neck down into my ribs, my ribs into those of the sofa-bed and howled like the damned who were being silenced. Was I really outraged by the death of this little girl whose path I had crossed a single time, one Sunday, that Sunday when a top was spinning inside my head? Was it having to count these dead again and realize that one of mine was among them? Traveling from so far only to find myself so low, crushed inside the slatted fences of a house that didn't even deserve the name, who wants that?

The bulb in one of the two lamps blew and I tried to sleep.

A few days later, it was Saturday. Janet's burial.

The little girl in the box looked like a plaster saint. When you walked up to her, she looked like Mary. You noticed the artificially rosy skin, the garish crown of artificial flowers across her forehead, her brushed hair shaped into a halo. If she had lived, her hair would have grown down to her waist and people would have declared, "blood doesn't lie." She would have waited until she was old before cutting it.

I inspected the rest. From the neck down, her beauty was gone. The body had swollen, looked like it weighed a ton. There were four who lifted the coffin. They were all dressed in black, except Paul whose tight, cream-colored pinstripe suit was clearly a bad idea. Two of the eight buttons on his double-breasted jacket, the two in the middle, had cracked open, letting you see everything he had on underneath: a silver chain with big links and a brown shirt also missing a button.

Relatives, friends, some neighbors rose from the benches to form a procession, but the porters had to pause to rest the weight they were carrying. The little one was refusing to leave.

That's what we would have thought, what we thought at home, when something so mysterious happened. When burying a man in the country over there, the coffin sometimes walked all by itself and only reached the cemetery after the deceased had paid off his debts. It had taken Caprice, my grandmother on my mother's side, a few days to reimburse debts. My mother told me how her coffin had suddenly opened up as the pastor began the mass, and how the old woman, not the person but her spirit, had run out of the church, then come to the village a week later to confess her sins. *Forgive me for pestering so-and-so, forgive me for stealing the husband of another, forgive me for eating the neighbor woman.* Dousing angers and being forgiven, that's what it meant to die clean.

I followed the flow when the church doors opened.
One man in a crowd.

A hundred of us moved down the street behind the deceased, the pallbearers, the family, the instruments and their players, all who'd come from Tremé to bury a child of Tremé. No longer was there the panic that had gripped bodies in the first hours after the accident. Now composed, those who were carrying, and those who came after, advanced slowly, dragging their feet like cinderblocks, marking the pace, 1-2 right, 1-2 left, 1-2 right, 1-2 left.

I am weak but Thou art strong, Jesus, keep me from all wrong,
I'll be satisfied as long as I walk, Let me walk close to Thee

Five men roused their brasses, two others made bass drums thunder, but the jazz that they played was beyond music. This jazz turned hearts toward the light, assured Janet a safe journey to the heavens, accompanied her to her final dwelling place, reminded all of us who followed, moving in lines to its rhythms, 1-2 right, 1-2 left, 1-2, right 1-2 left, that life didn't stop there, that in the end there was no end. I watched the marchers around me. They came from all sides. The street swelled, like a sea, filled wide, deep, with no beginning or end. Where would the procession end this morning? Its head had already reached St. Philip Street, Robertson, Villere . . . We would go all the way to the second Saint Louis Cemetery— the priestess Laveau lived in the first one—to depose Janet's embalmed corpse. Just a formality, since all together and at the same time we prayed sang cried marched to help her soul rise, save it from perpetual wandering or damnation. I was in the tide and let myself be carried by it.

I am weak but Thou art strong, Jesus, keep me from all wrong,
I'll be satisfied as long as I walk, Let me walk close to Thee

In the streets of old Tremé, the lament grew to a hurricane. It pushed open doors, dragged residents from their homes. Even the infirm rose up to dance in its arms. Even Mrs. Crouch, hey, I hadn't recognized her, even she was there in her wool socks, a short satin skirt, with an umbrella that served as a cane.

I'm not saying "Old Tremé" to show off. It's the expression that came to me as my fellow travelers, ahead and behind, all bid their farewells to little Janet according to custom, in the manner of those who had gone before, those who had arrived at the port of New Orleans three centuries earlier. They talked about a dozen boats loaded with captives. It was documented that most had come from Senegal and Mali. It's assumed that not many had survived the voyage. Many had fallen ill, which had meant death. Bodies had replaced other bodies. But, broadly, the customs had survived.

People were lined up in front of Janet's coffin. I waited my turn and tossed my rose on top of the forty-some flowers already covering it. No longer did I gaze at the coffin but at the family around it, the tear-streaked faces, the hands that consoled others and held handkerchiefs to mop faces before the release, the *Let it go*.

It seemed to take so long to get there. Seeing the Great Aunt Brenda again sent shivers down my back. More broken, devasted than the day of the accident. Older, just plain older. Her mouth was open, but her moans could not be heard. Paul was also among the mourners, no longer in his double-breasted jacket. Behind him, shorter by a head, Zaac clenched his jaw and his fists. If it hadn't been a battle against death, he would not have been convinced that he would lose.

It was the end, that is, a beginning. We let the soul go. I left the cemetery to follow the brass band that resumed the procession cheerfully. This time, they blew joy, all joy they blew. Everyone started shimmying, now all parts of the body: derrières, elbows, knees, hands, chest, feet. In front of me, a man had dropped to the ground and was slithering about like a snake. Further on, Mrs. Crouch's lace umbrella was waltzing around her. The ends of her bleached-blond locks fluttered from under her knit football cap. All would continue like this to the St. Augustine Church. At that point, the band would leave, the street would empty, and we'd wait for tomorrow for the count. Death is never free. My neighbor Mary, one of Janet's relatives, had gone from house to house to gather donations. There was so much money to collect, money for suits, money for food, money for the coffin, money for the jazz.

* * *

Lunch, which consisted of beer and jambalaya had long been consumed when Denim emerged from her house. I was still on Mary's porch when I saw her. She was hurrying toward her car, dragging a suitcase, hidden behind a pair of glasses with lenses so thick that there was no way to know what was going in on her heart. I watched her pull her suitcase whose wheels were being ruined by the cracks in the decaying sidewalk. She was parked near the spot where the ambulance had stopped to take Janet's body away. Death had struck a few just a few yards from her. She slipped an envelope to the little girl's parents and made a stop at the church, long enough for people to notice and be touched. After all, she didn't have to do that.

She loaded her suitcase in the trunk and excused herself. We were on the other side of the street, and she had to catch a plane for Dallas. "Dallas," Mary repeated dreamily, shifting her wig to rub her head. She was bald underneath it, and a fishbone scar divided her skull in two.

I asked her if she had already been there. She had only been out of New Orleans one time. That was after Katrina. Her brother had found her a job in a pharmaceutical factory in California. The work wasn't the greatest, but she had no regrets because she'd seen the Pacific Ocean. On Sunday, she'd get on the bus, treat herself to an ice cream cone, and spread her towel on the beach. The ocean wasn't made for swimming, she thought. She had never bought a swimsuit, never worn a pair of shoes that cost more than forty dollars, and never played poker, obviously.

She pushed her hairpiece into place, watching Denim start up her car. The two women were the same age. They'd known each other since nursery school. Mary chuckled. "I'm talking like a White person." There weren't any nursery schools at that time. The street was a family and we all belonged to it. The coupe drove off, but Mary was still staring at the pavement. "The only one behind us is God."

She went back to talking about the men's doings, to Paul's new plan to acquire a truck for selling Sno-balls. I imagined good old Paul in the driver's seat of his toy on wheels, complete with loudspeaker, loaded with shaved ice and syrups. Sno-balls were no small business here. They could make you king since everyone liked them. Wasn't a question of taste, but of a grudge. Eating and drinking a Sno-ball was proof that a person had been able to burn up the past, had left it far behind that night he set his pioneer feet and his muddy butt on this soil. Zaac had reminded me that, in the beginning, Americans were penniless. Yokels.

Mary, who got up to pour herself a glass, continued Paul's arguments. The syrups would pretty much be free, and there wouldn't be much competition, since some hoodlum had set fire to the biggest ice truck serving the neighborhood.

I'd heard about the fire and the vendor. The guy was nuts. He jacked up the volume of his loudspeakers while making his rounds. The music was a racist tune of the nostalgic Old South. "They're beasts. If you leave it up to them, they'll fight us again. You can't just accept everything," Zaac had told me.

A man came out of the house and sat down on the stoop. An accordion hung around his neck on fishing line. His forearms were tattooed and his teeth, fifty percent gold, fifty percent white, were distributed in his mouth like a checkerboard. I'd seen him at mass that morning, where he'd sung louder than the rest of us.

"These two, they're like husband and wife," Mary said, stroking the nylon line that attached the accordionist to his instrument. "They walk around glued to each other."

The man and the accordion had met when the man was still playing Boogeyman and hoops in the cane fields. As he grew up, he became a professional. He and the accordion became inseparable. They'd seen everything, the amazing and the pathetic. They had slept in the back of buses, sat in their section on trains, eaten what was put on their plate, occupied the lowest forms of housing, made people of all colors dance, then come back to Louisiana when the man felt too old to drag around.

"New Orleans will always be New Orleans!" Mary looked so proud when she said that, and so did the musician. She nodded, and he did too, hugging the accordion against his stomach like it was his own abdomen, there, where all pain and joy combined and altered each other. When he'd heard the news about Janet, he'd gotten up in the middle of the night to put together a little song. None of it referred directly to the little girl. His zydeco was a plain reminder that death is never savory.

"I made eight children in America, and those eight have made nineteen who have made nine others." As she counted, Mary wiped her eyes with the corner of the *popof* that she wore in the kitchen. She had sat down next to the accordionist whose forearm displayed a tattoo of a man, his throat slit, and stuffed into an accordion.

"Hey, Hardhead! You, French-speaker, why don't you sing this one with me?"

Mary seconded his request. She loved hearing me speak French. She said it sounded chic, and it made her relax. When she turned on the TV, she sometimes tuned into France 24. Out of courtesy to me, so I could listen.

My eyes met the gaze of the soloist with checkerboard teeth. He had wedged his accordion onto his thighs. He was ready.

Ô, je m'en vas Je m'en vas à la maison Tout seul, je n'ai pas conné où c'est Demander pour moi te voir Ô, je m'en vas M'en vas à la maison M'en vas, ô moi tout seul Quoi faire, c'est moi je vas à toi T'es après partir toi tout seul Ô, moi je m'en vas tous les samedis au soir Ô, je m'en vas à la maison . . .

I repeated the words shyly, then let him continue. In the third verse, the man all alone in the night was never able to get back home. He was caught by a gang of Whites who slit his throat. A sad affair. But God is great. The Black man survived. Someone found his body the next day and sewed up his throat.

Death is never savory, repeated the accordionist, death is never savory. He took up his old instrument and started the story again from another angle.

It was a Saturday night. The man whose throat would be cut had been invited to play at the home of some rich people. He was highly appreciated around here, because when he sang he emptied his whole soul into it. He was a musician. They didn't think about his color. He came, and as usual, he didn't just go through the paces. He played until he was sweating, soaking wet, so sweaty that a woman handed him her handkerchief. But this was the South. Seeing that, seeing a Black man touch a White woman's handkerchief could make heads explode.

When the evening is over, the all-alone man slides his accordion into a pillowcase and takes to the road for home. He's walking. A car pulls up behind him, he doesn't turn around. In the headlight beams lighting his path, he sees a little black something emerge and rear up on its back paws, and the man walking home alone wonders what a squirrel is doing out here at this hour. He keeps walking, the car still behind him, he feels the headlights on the back of his legs and backside, he can also hear the voices of the driver and passengers. There must be eight of them, or seven. Too many for a single car. The car drives past him, pulls over on the shoulder just ahead. On the right is the beginning of the dark, muddy bayou.

There are six of them. Five men and the White woman who had offered him her handkerchief. The man walking all alone thinks back to the squirrel sitting up on its back paws. Now he knows what the animal was trying to tell him. The five beasts approach, grab him by the feet and arms. One of them seizes the accordion, and to make sure it will never play again, jumps on it with his full weight and rage.

As it dies, the instrument emits a sound like giggling that will forever remain in the man's head, the man walking alone. The knife also makes a sound, a dry click. His throat, the target, bleeds. He drops to the ground.

Later, well after the five men plus the women have left, he will remember rolling the pillowcase around his neck and falling sleep in the wet grass.

The musician had stopped playing.

"What's the matter, Hardhead? We're just getting started and you've dropped out already. I asked you to sing along with me!"

"I'm not a singer."

"Oh, I'm not so sure of that," he said, stretching his instrument out to its full width. "Anyone who has suffered knows how to sing."

I was still pensive, stiff on my chair. What happened to the man whose throat had been sewn back up? Had the five men who had slit his throat been punished? And why was he calling me "Hardhead"?

"There's the man!" The musician hailed Zaac as he arrived, the bags under his eyes indicating that he'd been drinking or in a fight or crying. He'd done all three. That's all he'd done since the death of the little girl. He'd felt as wayward as a cloud. He admitted it, blaspheming like a man who'd been raised by the Devil, his speech was confused, we couldn't tell who he was calling a slut, the never-savory death that had taken Janet? The White woman who had held out her handkerchief when she knew what would happen? Or Amber, his pretty-faced little lady who'd had an affair with the boss at Whole Foods to end things?

Zaac sent the stool flying across the floor, the stool that Mary had gone to find him. It's not that he had no respect, but he'd had enough of this death that seemed to abuse only Black people. The hemorrhaging had to stop. They could build dams to keep out the sea, right?

The accordionist played a note in agreement, but Zaac took a dig at him.

"Keep your little oompahs to yourself. War isn't for clowns. You think you're a champ because you get gigs in the French Quarter, and with the bucks they give you, you can buy yourself a few beers? Go let your air out somewhere else, you and your little bandonion, and your scavenger music!"

And blah blah blah, on and on he spewed, even after the accordionist had cleared out, gone into the living room to withdraw from the altercation and take advantage of the feast. Blah blah blah, even when Paul and the others, who had spent the day eating, came up onto the porch, one after the other, trying to calm him down. Nothing worked. Fists clenched in an anger that was hardening, Zaac stood there in front of Mary's shotgun house. We needed an Amber, the Amber from before Whole Foods, to tamp down his anger or take him seriously. But a man without a woman was a man alone. A man without a family would always fight without a cause.

Mary stroked his cheek. "You'll be okay, you'll be okay." She'd seen me trembling behind the men while Zaac, after throwing punches for nothing, was dying of shame and exhaustion. She was someone I could ask why the man with gold teeth had nicknamed me Hardhead. A mother who'd raised eight children would know. But she turned away to be with Zaac, sure of herself and what only she could give him. She was going to tell him how handsome and kind he was, and in the face of all the blows he'd absorbed, fill him with what she alone could give him, which was unconditional love. That's what she gave him, then she helped him stand up and asked me to take care of him. She would have put him up that night, but all her beds were occupied. And with Brenda coming home from the hospital tomorrow . . .

She slowed down in the front yard to soothe the pain shooting through her legs. In the evening it always dragged her down a bit, but in the morning, all gone! She worked like an army. With the help of nobody, she cleaned her mama's helpless body and helped her out of her bedroom to air her out in front of the TV. Her mother had been the unmoving form in the bed that I'd seen on my first visit to Mary's house. Mary hadn't introduced me. I didn't know how many people lived in that house.

* * *

From how diligently Jeanne was urging me to take care of myself, I could tell that she was planning to leave me. To be honest, I was the one who had planted the idea. Since Janet's death, I'd held back from spending time online with her, skating past the intimate questions and only writing her cursory messages. After the little girl's burial, all sense of measure and compromise had abandoned me. Deep down, I was angry at Jeanne for not supporting me more and I accused her of acting like my mother whenever she took a step toward me. In the end, what I couldn't forgive her for was being a thousand leagues from Tremé and having neither Zaac's anger nor the limited destiny of the Crouch great-grandson.

So, Jeanne was going to leave, and this eventuality barely frightened me. All I could think of was sleep, how to get some sleep in this derelict bedroom with the sofa-bed that would not fold up, where Zaac was firmly installed, and snoring. At three in the morning, I gave up, slipped on a sweatshirt and jumped onto the bicycle that Mary had loaned me.

It had started to rain. I rode down the sidewalk, alone, totally conscious, *responsible* for my situation, to use Jeanne's word. On the ground, the rain turned holes into puddles that gleamed like little enchanted mirrors under the cognac light from the street lights. Garlands of electrical cords striped the columns on either side of front stoops. I imagined the lives behind the quiet facades, the accumulated happiness and unhappiness stacked up, contained in the rooms, boxes, cupboards. Everyone trying their best to cement it all together, so it would hold and not overflow. Had I been too hardheaded for this mason's dream to worm its way into my head and grow into an obsession? That's what I had believed and claimed until the age of thirty.

I pulled up my hood. With scaredy-cat speed, rode several blocks and stopped at that little business with no name, where everything seemed to arise from chance and human coagulation. People not yet absorbed by the night were there, squeezed in around dirty Formica tables or dozing between the aisles where medications, anti-mosquito sprays, birthday candles, soap, candy, pasta, toothpaste, chewing gum, coffee filters, coleslaw with or without mayonnaise were stacked up with no logic or labels.

I avoided the corner with the debaters and the table with people absorbed in board games and sat down near a young

woman who was busy sharpening a pencil and scribbling on
paper. From time to time, she looked up to respond to one of
the cashiers. She kept repeating "Muscatine" because the
cashier always asked her the same question. In the kitchen,
equipped with just a hot plate, fridge, and steam tables, where
a pot of black beans languished, a cook was repairing a five-
point soda machine by giving it a few shoves. The machine
only served Fanta, "the fucker!" Watching them both, an absurd
vision came to me of a peasant horsewhipping his jackass to
make it go, then a moment later being trampled by it.
Apparently, those animals could hold a grudge.

I ran my hand over my graying hair that the night drizzle
had nibbled, then pulled my notebook and the Evergreen
letters out of my sack and spread them out on the table. I was
looking for the passage where the planter's wife laments the
disappearance of a slave. I had started reading it the night I'd
slept at Jeri's house. But sleep had knocked me out, time had
flown, and it wasn't until this morning that the story of the
Evergreen runaway had come back to mind.

I took a sip of an Americano Aqueux and deciphered the
entire letter. They had set dogs, men, and horses to hunt down
the fugitive. They had searched the ground. Day and night,
they'd searched the woods and fields. Even dared to kill, to
make an example of him, to crush the desire of other captives
to flee. Two months after tracking him, a story had passed from
mouth to mouth, the runaway had been attacked by the giant
wolf Rougarou who had dragged him down under the bayou.

Rereading this story of the plantation and the bayou, I reflected on this incomprehensible ending to my uncle's life. Had he really come face-to-face with a man who had the head of a wolf? Was his death real or just a legend told to children who didn't want to go to bed? "The loup-garou is going to eat you!" That was the threat made to rebellious or turbulent children. To make them afraid. To bring them under control.

I looked up at the daughter of the Midwest who was asking me what I was working on. She was betting that I was a writer, and confirmed that she was one, she too, since she didn't always say the truth. She had lied to the cashier earlier, claiming to be a native of Iowa. She was actually from Houston and thought that if there was ever a godforsaken place where nothing happened, it had to be Muscatine. She chatted on, but I was no longer listening, wondering what would become of me when I went back to Paris. In a few weeks, I would be living in a furnished apartment and a neighborhood that I didn't know yet, I would greet new neighbors, I would come home every night from a pointless job, forgetting myself and this downtown drugstore-snack bar where I was beginning to feel sad and exhausted. Dully, I gathered up my belongings, turned in my tray, and pulled my hood up over my hard, dry head.

Outside, the rain was still coming down. Big drops, better to wait. Some of the bar customers tried to make quick escapes, covering their head with plastic bags, smokers took advantage of the chance to light up under the covered entrance, cockroaches continued their exodus toward the stuffed garbage cans, a poet, drunk as a sailor who was home on R&R, laid his cries at the feet of the coming overcast day. Searching the sky, I could see no opening, no divine halo there to soften the dawn. "A man dances on the moon, hops around the globe, then goes back underground," the prophet's song was fading into nature's din and the defeated city's shadows. It wasn't the cock's crow or the mourner's drone, I didn't know if death or life would come next.

The day was creeping forward like a frightened animal by the time I reached my room. I left the door open to let the day come in behind me and sat down on the sofa that Zaac, now in the shower, had figured out how to fold back up. It was really the only thing that we'd managed to do in this room that no cleaning woman had touched since I'd moved in. It would have taken a whole battery of cleaning products to annihilate the cockroach eggs, the filth that discolored the baseboards, the layer of grease on the walls, the human hairs everywhere and the skeletal remains of unidentified food remains behind the refrigerator. Denim, that good-for-nothing! She had signed and I had signed, but I was still waiting for a copy of the contract.

A shadow swelled on the disgusting wall perpendicular to the couch. Speak of the devil . . . Denim's handyman was standing by the sofa-bed, his telephone on speakerphone. He didn't need to explain why he was here, Denim was speaking for him. I could hear her accusing Zaac of stealing her car and ordering him to bring it back. She called him all kinds of names, as the little man with grandiose hands kept his eye on the bathroom door like an old tiger waiting to pounce on younger, but less clever prey. He had received the order to intervene if Zaac resisted. When the water stopped running, I warned Zaac that Denim was looking for him. I pictured these two belligerents forehead-to-forehead, the sharp features of the practiced crook vs. the unpretentious round nose of the wily handyman.

The gnome walked over to wait at the bathroom door. Right at the moment Denim ordered him to take action, we heard a slam. The small man dashed out the front door. In a split second, he had reached the sidewalk, but the young tiger had beaten him. He had escaped out the bathroom window and was starting his pick-up truck, tires squealing.

The sound of furniture being dragged around came from the house next door. Mary shook her mother: "Come on, now, let's be good!"

Later, sitting across from me, the gnome brooded, with a worried look, worry radiating from him, dimly illuminating the smudged page with information that Denim had dictated to him. He was waiting for her to call him back and for me to finish packing my bags. After Zaac's exit and his text message "Meet me in Baton Rouge," I had made up my mind to leave the bedroom in Tremé. I broke my lease and gave up my deposit without a fuss. And that's exactly what bothered Denim: not having to argue or be stingy. In a voice that trilled with haughtiness and pride, she concluded the deal. I was to leave the room spotless, just as I'd found it when I arrived. Her dwarf Josuah would make sure I did.

Now that his aging animal pulse had slowed, the gnome brought me sponges, a scrawny broom, and a box of baking soda. He handed me a pair of rubber gloves, then went back to inspecting the apartment with a close eye to report on its state at my check-out. "My Lisa is not a nasty woman. You just have to know how to handle her. You have to love her, that's all."

I studied the man. Not the slightest sign of ill-ease on his face. He calmly worked his way down the list, tapping his oversized thumb on the extra leaf in the table that was almost chest-level for him. He slipped the document into his pants pocket and unbuttoned his jacket with shoulder pads, the one he'd worn to the ball at the Hyatt Hotel and which made his arms look like tree limbs. I was always thrown off by his stumpy legs. What made him attractive to Denim? What did she see in him? The more I watched him, the less I understood.

* * *

It was early afternoon, Josuah was preening in Denim's limousine, windows down, driving slowly, slowly to make sure people would take note and show him respect. Tremé being only two miles from the Union Passenger Terminal, he took his time, really all his time to roll down Loyola Avenue, pause at all the red lights and yield to pedestrians, including those who weren't crossing.

I would have preferred to sit up front, but he seated me in
the back and, *to avoid disturbing the client,* had turned the car
radio down low. Cleaning the shack together had not made
us equals. Deep inside, the unskilled worker was taking pleasure in what he was: a former errand boy, promoted to the rank
of subordinate authorized to perform all kinds of chores and
benefit from certain privileges. Through these odd jobs and
symbolic bonuses, Denim maintained her hold on him and on
her people. She didn't pay a salary, her governance was based
on a feudal system in which money played only an incidental
role. Zaac, by receiving his pay directly, by depriving her of
her dollars, had violated the rules.

We arrived at the bus station. Josuah parked the limo and
insisted on opening my door and dragging my big suitcase on
wheels to the counter where I bought a one-way ticket. I took
my bag from him with an awkward thank you. Was he hoping
that I would pat him on the back and slip him a bill, even a
small one? I yielded to custom, everything cost money down
here, then entered the station where about fifty travelers were
sitting, gear at their feet, snack packages in their hands, ready
to depart for Austin, Pensacola, Houston, Memphis, El Paso,
Jacksonville, Atlanta, Baltimore, Portland, as soon as their bus
number lit up on the Departures board.

I'd never been to any of these cities, but looking at the
faces of those who were headed there, I wanted to believe that
they were the finest corners of the world, where families
greeted their own with plates of meat that had been cooking
all night long, nice tablecloths and napkins, a fire they would

light when the temperature dipped, when an uncle, to set the evening's rhythm would start singing, "Mother Banana: Why didn't you go to school today? Little Banana: Because I didn't peel well." Everyone would laugh at the banana joke and call for more.

Where families were a unit, despite bad luck, running short on money, the ups and downs of an existence never chosen, but what could you do? That's where I wanted to go. To sit among people I didn't know, long enough to make myself anew. Surely, there would be a place for me. Make yourself at home, they said.

I found a hot-drink machine, slid my last bill into the slot, and put my ear to the machine to hear the instant coffee with powdered cream being prepared inside it. The machine shut off just as the plastic cup had filled to the top and a voice over the loudspeaker announced "Baton Rouge, Baton Rouge."

There were only seven of us in the bus, practically all men. The only woman was the driver and the only two not dozing were two men who were quibbling. Their circular reasoning and monotone voices reached me in scraps. They had been speechifying, since the bus had started up, on the expression "playing music." One of them said, "There's playing music and living music . . . You can't understand a musician if you've never seen him on stage . . . a musician lives when he plays . . . a musician doesn't just play, he breathes." The more they agreed, the more they squabbled.

Lake Pontchartrain. We were crossing the bridge. Through the window, I contemplated what remained of the cypress trees. Their slow, emaciated bodies were gray with moss. Their carcasses were collapsing like the shadows of the elderly. I watched a flock of white egrets patrolling the area like a team of lifesavers rescuing the drowned. A heavy shower stole my view of them. The driver flipped on the windshield wipers. "Damn condensation!" We glided along blind. She tempested against the downpours that let loose just anytime, never played by the rules. She thundered again when the rain moved on and the sun came back, so radiant that it created mirages. I pressed my face against the window to watch the sky change. No longer bottled up, it turned mauve, indigo, green, yellow, purple. It had transformed into a rainbow, lazily arching its back over the lake. In the soothing silence of the return to clear air, I felt a stab of nostalgia and thought of Ngan Medza, the python of all pythons who had allowed my Beti ancestors to step over River Yom to escape their enemies.

When Garoua's cousin sang about this saga, images wide as frescoes paraded through my head. I imagined the Beti people chased from their village by faceless beings dressed like rock stars. They fled south until a river cut off their path. Now what? He-who-forged-man took pity on them. Striking the river with his magic wand, he summoned the python-rainbow, and all my ancestors climbed onto its back. The story dated from the time when they offered sticks of sugar to the ghosts to feed them, and offered ivory to the foreigners. Ivory in exchange for rifles. And the rifles had emboldened the men to sell men to other men.

We were still on the bridge. The rainbow was fading. Once again, like a thirsty receptacle, the sky was filling with water. I was thinking, they're going to catch us. I wanted to urge the driver, "Faster! Faster!" and tell her the story about the python's act and the living ghosts who lived underground, down where the earth is soft, and from where they rose and sank back down again. They did everything the opposite of us, and owned lions that meowed like cats. "Faster!" or they would take us down where man meets his death.

At the driver's crisp *watch your step*, I changed my mind and stayed in my seat until the last stop, until Florida Boulevard, which was so dismal that I reread Zaac's directions to make sure I was in the right place.

A dilapidated Mustang rattled up to the sidewalk, backfiring. Inside, I identified Jeri, who'd come to pick me up with Alex, a large body topped with a child's head, squeezed into the back seat. The boy muttered the beginnings of a hello, then stuck his earphones back in his ears. I wedged my bag into the trunk, already crammed full, and arranged my legs as well as possible in the old clunker. The floor on my side was a jumble of books and rumpled newspapers. I opened the conversation by asking what's new. Jeri answered with a resigned pout. Her car, barely three years old, had croaked, so she'd had to bring out the old mule, a strange beast with sheepskin seat covers, a garland of plastic flowers lying on the ledge inside the rear window, two white rabbit's feet hanging from the rearview mirror, and a lace steering-wheel cover. Most spectacular was the ceiling, carpeted with photos of black celebrities, photos cut from magazines. Everybody was there, overhead: men and women, the dead and the living, people and martyrs, America, Europe, the Caribbean, and an African section that Jeri seemed proud of, though

I wasn't sure why. Not much there. Just two portraits of Lumumba, the real one and the actor in the Raoul Peck film.

For a moment, a memory came back to me, the time when I had beat up a classmate because he'd called the leader of the Congolese independence movement a hypocrite. It was my first fight, with everything you need for a fight when you're a kid: a school yard, spectators on both sides, the punch you didn't see coming, the fear of not knowing how to fight, a voice barking "Fight, if you're a man," a voice from inside making you crazy and strong. Yeah, I'm a man! Yeah! And from there you punch and punch again. Victory. You're the best. Hands clap with joy, arms lift you up, the sky swings about when your friends change direction, a smile from the prettiest girl in the class, walking home with the gang, retelling the fight for the twentieth time to those who weren't there, to those who were in the back or too far away to see, the twentieth time you retell it to yourself, especially before falling asleep in a state of bliss. I was suspended for committing violence and not respecting discipline. When asked why I'd been punished, I told people it was political. In my own eyes, I was a rebel.

In the Mustang, its ceiling paved with heads of gods, Jeri scolded Alex for the racket that he was listening to at full blast on his iPad. She refused to refer to her son's music any other way. Maybe she knew nothing about today's singers. Maybe she was an old-fashioned mother, but still. What was streaming out of the earphones purchased with her savings went against the values that she was breaking her coconut to try to pass onto him. Alex unscrewed his mouth to rebel, but that was too much, it was the kick that Jeri had been waiting for to stop the car and dump everything out on the sidewalk: book bag, iPad, teenager. She revved the engine, shot off without looking back. Not her problem if the house was fifty-three minutes away at a trot, or if the teenager was wearing jeans that were too light-colored to be walking in the dust. In my day, a young man knew how to hold his tongue, in my day, she repeated, punching the phone number of her diabetic Aunt Joe, a young man knew his place. I let her talk in circles, pushing the Mustang as hard as she could, then parking in front of a colorful house that looked like a pair of patched jeans.

That's how I found myself at the Wests' kitchen table, seated between Auntie Joe—Joe, for Josephine, an old woman built like a parallelogram, with mottled skin—and her husband, Martin the rice eater. Joe was engrossed in the instruction manual for a fruit slicer, won in a game show on television. Her good sense and experience as a housewife led her to conclude that the gadget worked only for apples. She peeled three Pink Ladies to demonstrate. She had the way of those who accommodate themselves to whatever is given to them. I had told her my first name and she used it with no frills. "What do you think, Nathan?" "Make yourself at home, Nathan." She showed me how to operate the apple slicer. "You just press once and poof! It cuts."

She got up to wash her hands and then settled her hindquarters on the seat, where they ballooned out past her hip bones. The torture chair, where Jeri injected her with insulin once a week. During that time, Martin rustled up two cups of coffee and showed me around the place, a quasi-irrational living space. We passed through four rooms to reach the bathroom, we walked through the garden to reach the storeroom, we ducked down to go through the too-low doorway to the kitchen which was nothing more than the extension of the first room. During the ninety-five years of its existence, the owners had just kept adding more square feet to the house and shifting the furnishings, like the bookcase where Dr. Seuss books were gathering dust. *Green Eggs and Ham, The Cat in the Hat, One Fish, Two Fish, Red Fish, Blue Fish.* All American children had read these stories. Seuss had died a rich man.

A young man in a dashiki and impeccably white shoes entered the living room. He was Marvin, Joe's youngest child, still excited by his *"phenomenal, guys!"* evening in New Orleans. He was online with two friends as he told us about the crowd that had come to the Ashé Center the night before to celebrate the release of a former Black Panther. "Forty-three years in prison, it's unbelievable. They just let him out three days ago, those bastards!"

Joe didn't object to the swear words. What she wanted was for her son to act with prudence. Her blood pressure shot up every time he went out for the evening, and every time the phone rang.

Later, when we got back into the Mustang, Jeri would remember her aunt's first son, September 18th, 2009, when she had been the first one a neighbor called at dawn, she—Jeri—to tell her that the boy was lying on the ground, in the middle of the street. Jeri had stammered her cousin's name to be sure there was no mistake, and asked "What do you mean, lying? What do you mean, dead?"

Had she been told what had happened? Had the police treated Joe like a lady? Is it possible to survive the death of your child?

I listened to the story and was left unsure. Being dismayed wasn't enough. I also wondered in what kind of country I had landed. I saw death jerking with death right before my eyes, corpses limping down a boulevard of dried blood, I understood that America is not a new country but an old world that has never been washed clean. No one has prayed for it. It has never been punished. It has never been castigated.

* * *

Aunt Joe shouted, see you soon. I watched Jeri slam the car door, her hands impatient to get the steering wheel moving, her classic straight skirt, her pretty legs, finally, the stubborn, energetic face she put on over the real one to make her look composed. She worried about Zaac, she'd never seen so close to bottom. She'd told him that he could stay at her house, that's what you do for a friend, but nobody can make anybody do anything. It was up to Zaac to decide.

"What about you, when are you going home?"

She turned on the radio and I felt her bitterness surge again. With all these black faces right over our heads, these beautiful black faces glued to the ceiling, I had some nerve getting involved. Shit, did I have amnesia or something? What was burning in my belly instead of my brain? Under her hard stare, judgmental as a decree, I again felt a wave of shame roll through my body, a physiological confusion that cut into my tongue and the back of my knees. I was the trapped rat, and Jeri, the poacher watching me squirm.

"I haven't been lynched, Jeri."

"We all have been."

"No dog has ever chased after me to chew up my ass. My grandmother was never called Rosa Parks. I have never had to run for my life from the South, I don't know that South. All I've done is read, and suffer in a way that will never be yours. I have no memories of the men in pointed hoods who made Tanti Joe's mother tremble with fear or fury. I'm a European African. That doesn't mean much, except maybe that I also sleep with White women."

Jeri accelerated, and there was nothing left but the road. The sound of tires on asphalt and the modulations of a crooner on the radio, lamenting the impermanence of love. I told myself, this is just how it was with Jeanne, and ran back through our last phone call and the last six years of our conjugal life with a sorrow that made me angry. It seemed like the two had lasted about the same amount of time. I had gotten mixed up with a woman and the mixing had lasted for about five minutes.

I looked up at the ceiling where Malcolm X, invited to give a lecture in Paris, was walking down a sidewalk in the 5th arrondissement. I was very familiar with this photograph, taken in the mid-1960s. Long ago, I had pinned it up on the wall in my bedroom, along with the portrait in which the militant had been refused entry to France at Orly Airport by the French police. It happened a few months after the first meeting at the Maison de la Mutualité. Malcolm left again, calling Paris Johannesburg, they were one and the same. He had encouraged the Black communities of the world to rally against their oppressors.

I was imagining Jeri, kneeling on the back seat of her Mustang with a pair of scissors and a box of 100 thumb tacks. If Malcolm X had still been alive, I would have laughed out loud.

We arrived at Jeri's place where Zaac was swinging in a hammock, looking like he was thinking ahh, vacation! Or, To the good life! He didn't fool us, Jeri or me, but after what had happened in her car, we rolled with Zaac's tall tales, Zaac, who prided himself in bilking Denim for all these years without ever being nabbed by her handymen. "I'm not a thief, I'm a revolutionary!" and in unison we answered, of course. We pretended to be relaxed but avoided looking at each other. Neither one of us wanted to start in again.

That evening, Auntie Joe's son Marvin insisted on taking us to his university, where his new hero, the former Black Panther, was giving a talk. He had borrowed his father's minivan so he could take as many people as possible. There were at least fifteen of us in the vehicle, of all sizes, all ages, squeezed in like herrings.

In the lecture hall, it felt like being in church during the singing of the psalms. The same exaltation, when the host, who addressed the audience like a rousing priest, asked us all to welcome *our brother* who had burned through more than half of his life in a place where daylight never penetrates, a solitary-confinement cell at Angola. Some shed tears, others raised their fist as the convict-made-saint walked to the stage, supported by his brother who was smiling for both of them. For the man was exhausted.

He took a seat, and the room exploded into applause. "A standing ovation for our brother," hammered the host, a hand-kerchief to wipe off sweat thrown over his shoulder. The temperature was rising.

"How you doing?" The hero had to start somewhere. He began with the epilogue, his release from prison, and his stomach that he couldn't wait to fill at Li'l Dizzy's Café on Esplanade. The host knew the place. "They have the best Trout Baquet in the world." Trout, yep, that's exactly what the man had ordered, and he'd spent the day, his first day out from behind bars, at this dive in the Tremé district, with tables that he said were always filled and a line outside that stretched for blocks. "Some people stand outside for two hours, just to eat there. Stand outside and not a single parasol."

He piled on the anecdotes and alluded to his state of health, his legs messed up by the cages. Those cells are a box. You take one step and *bam*, there's the wall, you stand up and *bam*, there's the ceiling. But don't worry, he'd be back to his old body in no time. Soon, we'd see him shaking a leg all over town, running races and winning.

The man stood up and raised his fist. That's all we could see, his clenched fist at the end of his arm, this was no longer one man's fist but the heart of a community eternally enraged because eternally cheated.

Could this be repaired?

I was watching, I was trying to look at the man with the iron faith and shriveled thighs. He had sat down again and was mopping his face. What was he going to do with his life now? When you're old, life is for the everything that's good: eating a po'boy, thinking, damn that's good, swallowing an icy black beer, staying with a woman because she knows how to cook, lifting one cheek to pass wind, stretching out in a park to roll a ciga-rette, listening to soft music on a hotel balcony, falling asleep, waking up feeling lively, going boating on a lake, playing pool, having a cookout, driving a monster car with one hand and rolling down the window to feel the rain.

I would have liked to believe him, believe that everything would be fixed. That you could teach a clenched fist to dance again. I would have liked to be a man who had never cried, but in that hall all the guys were outraged. Fuck justice! Fuck the United States of America! Fuck the police! Their hands curled into a ball, hard as a stone.

To calm the crowd and appease the mounting swell of fury, the host, who had been a Panther, reminded everyone of his brothers' program. In New Haven, they'd given bread to the poor, dreams and schools to children. Every day, they had fought to improve the lives of families. In that Connecticut city, trans-formed into their general headquarters, they had understood this: economic justice comes first. "Seriously, what good is the right to enter a restaurant if you don't have the money to pay for a meal?"

Things were happening in the rows of seats. Everybody pushing to get up to the stage and take the mic.

"My father is always targeted by the cops," declared a student who had mounted a chair. "My grandfather was targeted by the cops, my great-grandfather was targeted by the cops, my great-great grandfather was targeted by the cops . . ."

To the point where, when the student sat down at church, it wasn't to pray for a good life, a job, a family, a trip around the world in a car with open windows. He prayed hard just to finish the year still standing, not to be shot behind some apartment building or on television before Christmas.

He continued, "I saw Rekia Boyd, Eric Garner, Tamir Rice get killed on TV." The hero from the Panthers wiped his eyes. "It was on every channel, free of charge, open to the public, just like when they used to lynch us."

Entire rows of people were chanting *The New Jim Crow!* The student nodded his agreement. In his room, he kept a pistol within reach in case someone broke in during the night, in case the police decided to finish him off too, or in case things got rough. In case he had the desire to press the revolver to his temple and pull the trigger.

I remembered Davis from Cousin's BBQ in Dallas and the grandson he adored like a church relic, I felt Jeri falter, her mother's body crack. The student had said it: fear and despondency were now embedded in their genes.

Jeri straightened up in her seat, excusing herself, but I acted like I didn't understand. We couldn't hear each other in this cursed uproar, anyway. The host congratulated the hero, the brother thanked the audience, the old soldier said his last remarks, their voices rose one above the other, drowned out by the voice of the student who was standing on his chair with a microphone and a bundle of tracts protesting police brutality.

I left Zaac and followed Jeri to the campus gates where a sisterhood of students in heels was rippling toward a white building set deep in the night. To the right was the lake that stretched along the road and then ended at the municipal park. A while ago, I'd seen ducks floating there. Students jogging along the shore.

Now the water was alone.

I walked over to the bank while Jeri was trying to reach her son. I leaned out to catch the scent, the breath of the lake. Inside me, I felt it flowing inside me and filling my soul, drop by drop. I inhaled, emptied myself, inhaled and emptied myself until I felt dizzy. My pulse had slowed, I went down on my knees and touched my forehead to the ground. Like a man who believes, I bowed down to the river.

I've known rivers
I've known rivers ancient as the world and older than the flow
of human blood in human veins . . .

The frogs croaked to these lines of the Langston Hughes poem I recited in a low voice. They were celebrating the Euphrates, the Nile, the Congo, and the billions of miles that the world had walked to become this world. According to the story, Hughes had written this poem on a train while crossing the Mississippi to find his father. I wished I had the guts to swim across it, this body of water reddened by so many iron chains and so many tears of the enslaved. I could barely find the strength to pick myself up.

I caught up with Jeri and adjusted my step to hers so I could stop thinking. Didn't work. As I walked, I opined on everything, I droned on about thoughts that led to nothing. I said thank you, then good riddance to Lousiana, to Zaac, and to this woman who, wanting to save all the brothers who slept with White women, was probably plotting to convert me into I didn't know what kind of black god or martyr.

Jeri stopped in her tracks. She was standing in front of a rundown Victorian house, her arm pointing at the roof. "Look, opossums. They're coming from up there." All I could see were shingles. "Look, those are even bigger than the others."

We were a block away from her place and her shotgun. If we ran home, grabbed the gun and came back, we couldn't miss them. But Jeri hesitated. The opossums who were clever as humans wouldn't wait for the first shot to scram. So, she brought her two hands together, arms stretched out in front of her, and not breathing, took aim at the roof. The shingles crackled. Jeri holstered her imaginary piece, and we went on our way, she ahead, me behind. Her body was now just a figure of exhaustion making its way home.

* * *

We arrived just as Alex was downing his last serving of sausage pasta bread Sprite. He gave me a little nod of acknowledgement and ignored his mother's awkward attempts to bring him into the conversation. He poured himself another glass of soda, washed his dishes, then disappeared into his room which soon began to emit throbbing music that buzzed around the room like zonzons. I had only been there a few hours and already this house had a hold on me, enmeshing me in its moods and small dramas. The first time I'd been invited, everything seemed clear-cut and simple. I had dropped onto the sofa, swathed in alcohol and music.

Jeri set the table with two plates that she filled with meat and leftover okra in sauce given to us by her Aunt Joe. We weren't waiting for Zaac. Marvin had called to say he would bring him by tomorrow. I forced myself to eat the vegetables, but left the meat, even though my stomach was growling. Across from me, Jeri was devouring enough for three. Like mother, like son, she ate as much as Alex. As she was inhaling her last mound of food, she lifted her chin from the plate and studied me: "I want to show you something, but first, I need to know if I can trust you."

I hesitated. I hadn't reacted when Jeanne, before hanging up, reminded me how hard she had fought to keep me. A grin of disgust formed naturally as I imagined her efforts. I had watched her tow us along to keep our life as a couple moving straight ahead. Jeanne as beast of burden. At least it confirmed that she was dependable. I looked at Jeri staring at me and wondered what she was reading in my eyes. How did I know if

I was dependable or not? No one had ever counted on me. And I had given so little.

I nodded anyway, and Jeri's face broadened suddenly, like a moon when you notice it's full. She jumped up to make boiling-hot tea, and in a flash we were in her room, sprawled on cushions, facing a wall entirely covered with photos. Some were color, some black-and-white, some blown up, some tiny, pictures of people, places, things that had moved Jeri during her rare travels.

"Some call that Lovely Cool," she murmured, pointing at a series of photos, all taken in the same village. "Others prefer to call it La Vilokan." Squeezed between two rivers in northwest Haiti, the village that Jeri showed me had become a place of pilgrimage, which she described with eyes closed as she pictured it. "Over there is the first voodoo temple. Not the one people know, but the very first one, where the first runaway slave took refuge. Now, don't think of a big temple with earthen walls, don't think of drums. There, they used hands to accompany the voices, the women sang, the women prayed. I don't know where the men were. I assume they came later. Going into the temple, I noticed the curtain right away. It wasn't very big but seemed so thick and heavy, as if there were other curtains behind it, as if just on the other side was the Energy, and all you'd have to do was lift the curtain. Behind all those curtains layered on top of one another, I felt Guinea with such force. I had found all the strength of the ancestors, the strength that had been taken from us."

I took note of the corrugated sheet-metal temple and other photos: the masses of pilgrims, heads moored in simple scarves, mouths of beggars, begging for relief from their struggles, for help from the divinity. There was Jeri and women dancing, Jeri and the guide, Jeri and the priest, Jeri and her Black body on vacation. Walking in a country where the Black person is just a person, that's what Haiti was, first and foremost.

"I spent two nights in the village, and do you know what I learned? That the first runaway was a woman. Can you believe it?"

She pressed her cup of lemongrass tea to her lips and in a voice that came from deep down in her gut, groaned, "Oh, how I hurt!" She felt heavy with the troubles that piled up like the temple curtains. She would not be healed. Things aren't repaired, they're just patched up.

I reached out to take her in my arms: "Guinea loves all her children. Guinea has not forgotten you." In that moment, I wanted to be an envelope, a shell, a cradle for this afflicted woman, I wanted her to turn over a few crumbs of her pain over to me, the African, as I was known in Tremé. I would know what to do with it, I would scatter them at the mouth of a river.

Jeri was as tense as a trapped animal. Her arms resisted mine, water spilled from her eyes. I hugged her tighter and stroked her hair. A brotherly gesture in the face of the troubles and the great dispersion.

Much later, after having put her to bed, I sat down close to her to tell her the story of the woman who had escaped from Evergreen, the one I'd read about in the old letters that Lewis, the archivist, had entrusted to me. Naturally, I exaggerated. The runaway slave had returned to haunt the plantation. Her voice could be heard whistling above the big house, a voice like a horsehair whip. It was said that her shadow could be seen going up-down the stairs, her stride swift, 123 steps to the kitchen, light the fires, bite the livestock animals until they bled. She was the iron dog, the cane toad, the masters' affliction.

"No question she was the runaway of La Vilokan. She'd left Louisiana forever and come home." Jeri's hypothesis had legs. For over two centuries, Haiti and Louisiana had been engaged in an off-kilter dance together.

Exhaustion fell over us, but we clung to the spoken word. The tale was our canoe. We were going from one bank to the other, invincible, deaf to the bedlam in the world, to the chaos of the opossums, and the sirens that split the night. We were brother and sister. Together, we were tugging on this story by its longest thread, weaving the tale of that runaway slave uprooted from Guinea, that part was decided, enslaved in Haiti and that her master had packed her in his trunk when he fled to Louisiana.

In her diary, the wife of the planter indicated that the rebellious woman had escaped from the plantation right at the start of the Spanish-moss harvest. We were reinventing the time and reasons for her disappearance. After years underground and underwater, the escapee had returned to Haiti to look after the temple and the treasure behind the curtains.

When Jeri slipped her warm hand into mine, I thought of my mother, how much I had missed her body. She had stopped protecting me as soon as we were established in Paris. "You're not a girl." Each time I needed her, her breasts, her lap, she scolded me. "You're not a child anymore." What was I then? Outside, they called me the Negro.

Outside, beyond the French doors, the sun was still on its knees, scrubbing the city of Baton Rouge. A scarlet band had cut the world in two, down below was the filth, up above, the hovering sky. But the day would win out, would return with its gang, its usual. In the garden, the wind was tickling the treetops. The first birds tried out their voices.

* * *

I left the bedroom and went to sit outside, behind the house, on the unfinished terrace. Jeri was planning to pave it. She had purchased the tools and slabs of natural slate. All that remained was to recruit Alex and get started. Feeling a hairy mass rub against my calves, I leaped up and pulled my chair away. A cat shot off behind the wall of bougainvillea turning purple in the dawn's light.

What was I going to do with the last three weeks left to me here? That night had revealed the vanity of my quest. I needed to leave the dead and the buried legends under the ground, take up life again and allow those disappeared to depart.

It seemed like someone was talking to me. I looked up but saw no one. I was alone. It was all in my head, where my father's words still echoed. Twenty-eight years ago, walking me to the door, putting me out, putting me out of his house in Bastos, he'd said, "In a family, there are those who leave and those who stay." I was the one who had left. He had stayed. I was not welcome in his house. From now on, I belonged to the great outside world. I walked with the wind.

Etienne John Wayne Marie-Pierre left Douala in July 1946. He died twice, as they say. No one today can bring him to mind or sing his deeds. In our family, he is nothing more than a compound first name. If he'd stayed in the country, he would have become a branch of the tree, certainly not this bit of driftwood, rejected by the ocean, currents, and coincidences. I'd never seen a photo of him. I imagined that we resembled each other some, he and I, and that we were equally monstrous. Wandering disfigures a man.

The sliding glass door from the living room eased open. Alex walked toward me with a big glass of soda and some bread. Without his fluorescent-green earphones and his scowl, he had a standard face. He was the kind of boy who needs some time to grow handsome and is well liked by girls when they begin to smooth their rough edges.

He sat down and grabbed the cat by the tail, the cat who had come back and was under the table together with two others. Under this torture, the animal purred. "He's a boxer," explained Alex who had named him Boxer while he waited for his mother to poison it.

He shook his head. "My mother is a radical." He let the animal go and stretched his arms out as if getting ready to take off, as if there weren't a wall in front of us, but a sun perched on the ocean. "Me, I'm just me," he added, pulling his chest in. "She's the one who thinks I take after my father."

Because Jeri had never mentioned this man's existence, I had naively assumed that he was dead or in prison. I felt shamefaced listening to Alex's cursory description of him. His father was a conservative at ease in the system. "He profits. No shame there."

He leaned over to resume his boxing match with the feline, and I mulled over this phantom-father. I didn't know if he'd lived there, if he had his heart set on making his son happy. I didn't dare ask. I would have had a better idea of how to deal with a small child, talk about his favorite teddy bear, his teacher at school, or what he wanted to be when he grew up.

Boxer leaped out from under the table and sprang toward the low wall, now a lizard racetrack. Seeing so much prey all at once and unable to catch anything made the cat belligerent and sour. He meowed, frustrated, extending his paw and ignoring Alex's teasing, and the barks coming from Alex's mother.

"She treats her cats better than her husband," Jeri said about her neighbor. As soon as she woke up in the morning, she slipped on her robe to go feed them. The meat that she served them twice a day came from the butcher. Which explained the raccoons, the opossums, and the cancan on the roof.

Alex was in a sociable mood. At school, they'd shown a Truffaut film. Did Paris still look like that, a city with Whites sitting around gabbing and drinking coffee?

I reflected on the attraction that Paris had held for Black American intellectuals. After being turned away from a restaurant, Baldwin had sought refuge over there. The deciding factor wasn't a fear of dying, but rather the certainty that if he didn't leave the country now, he would give in to his rage. He would kill the waitress who refused to serve him, the driver who refused to drive him, the policeman who refused to protect him, the pastor who refused to bless him.

What had the writer thought of France during all those years he lived there? Had he seen the Arabs thrown in the Seine, the Jews accused of trafficking in White slaves, the Africans imported by France whenever needed, the Antilleans brought to replace Algerians when they were declared Algerian again? Had he militated against the BUMIDOM, the shantytowns where Italians, Portuguese, Spaniards were shunted, before being boxed up in apartment blocks? If he were still alive and in France, would he still be cool and naive, a Black American who didn't feel his anger rising because he had come from afar? Truffaut was cinema. But how could I admit that to a young man who dreamed of taking flight?

I talked about the bars where all sorts of people mingled, the old record shops, the old used-book sellers, the old stone, the Apple Store near the Opera, the sneaker store where you design your own shoe, the Indian shopkeeper's mangoes imported by jet, the corn porridge in Château-Rouge, the banks of the Seine, covered with a thick layer of sand in summer to create a beach, create vacations, the New Morning venue where I'd seen Shepp play—an explosive concert! Especially when the tambouyé Guy Konket, rest his soul, had come back up on stage to accompany the American. Drum plus sax, a class act. *Plakpatapkpatakplak tootdooddoddogonggongonggongontooloo* . . . I imitated the sound of the instruments.

In the category of eateries, I recommended Galerie 88, not for the number of stars but for the view, the best in Paris. When you sat on the burgundy-red benches in the booths, you saw the river, the bateaux-mouches if you liked to watch them glide along, but more importantly the girls with those legs, which the wind revealed each time it ruffled their skirts. It had become a ritual. Once a week I showed up there, from 3 to 5, when the light was ideal. And the food? Simple but tasty: a bean soup like they serve in Tangier, sesame bread and tagliatelle. "You'd die because you're wild about pasta!"

Alex was already imagining himself over there in a tea salon in the 4th arrondissement. It was Paris, but could have been Berlin or London, as long as he could walk around alone or with a few friends. Four friends, same background, same color, so what? What difference would that make? Who would worry about that? Walk freely in a pack, go into clubs and bars, and shout, "Waiter, a beer!" or something stronger. Trail around with no worries about the time or neighborhood limits, without your heart tingling if a police car slowed or a man who didn't know him from Awa or Adam demanded to see his papers.

Feeling like the earth had no ceiling.

The day dawned with this hope.

They were expected in late May. But this year they came early, mercilessly soaking the earth for a week already. Not surprising that the Cajuns called them *avalasses*. Sticky, clammy air had come with the waters. Staying clean was a fantasy. Clothes stuck to the skin. All day long until dusk, the sky looked the same, thick and gray as an army blanket.

We no longer heard the neighbor, or her cats, or the tap dance of rodents on the roof. Alex's school had closed. Every day, Zaac's phone warned of flooding. Floods everywhere. Curfew at 9 p.m. State of emergency, police sirens, ambulances. Resigned and ready, residents wished one another good luck. They remembered that luck could turn bad. Last time, New Orleans had had it rough.

The danger also came from below, when the bayous and the waterlogged soil unleashed their beasts. Aunt Joe had found six brahminy blindsnakes in her toilet bowls. These burrowing snakes are not odious. They are no longer than a man's foot and not venomous, but the old woman slammed the lid down in a panic. Scrubbed the room down with holy water and bleach, then, crossing herself, howled at Satan and the feckless angels.

"I'll get 'em out!" Zaac swore. Since the incident, Zaac slept, when he slept, with a machete across his heart, and kept repeating the story, though it was known to all, the story of how Mr. Reynold had poisoned a coral snake, two yards long, with fox piss and Snake Stopper.

The local television news had shown Reynold holding up the entire dead snake. He hadn't damaged it because "a long one is always a good sign. When the earth is purified, the snakes come out and our sins are washed away."

For Zaac, it was the rattlers. No question, if he came across one he would hack it to pieces. He'd had enough of all the tales peddled by Reynold, the neighbors—everybody around here, including Jeri. He was sick of them, and to put an end to this discussion that resurfaced every day, he drifted to the sofa, stared at the fan and counted aloud the number of blades per second.

But Jeri, who was so fond of taking the floor, only ceded it when Zaac, the miscreant, folded and admitted that she was right. Then she slipped on her boots, rain slicker, and hat, shouted see you later and never got any farther than the bougainvillea hedge.

Watching her empty out her socks in the kitchen sink, I wondered what sins the residents of this city had committed to be cursed with so much rain and so many snakes. To get

some idea, I kept studying the sky, up where men pay their
debts. The war between God and Devil was everlasting.

To counteract the nasty, Jeri burned sticks of lavender and
white sage. I heard her striking matches, try again, swear. Every
day, she swore she'd buy a lighter, since water is fire's enemy.

A few days after the snake incident, nobody at Jeri's was
putting on a brave face anymore. We stood around Alex's bed,
anxious, silent—worried by the nightmare he'd had, which
had awakened us all. From his screams, I'd thought I was
hearing a thousand hyenas. I rushed to his room where Zaac
was already standing, still clutching his *cut-cut*. Jeri, shaken, was
there too.

Alex had seen himself hanging from one of the oak trees
whose limbs stretch and arc down to the ground, with
branches like tentacles. These trees grew in profusion in the
city park where men and women pushed strollers and walked
dogs. That was people's life here: take a walk, take in some fresh
air while the trees made shade.

The oak trees, too, continued to breathe easily, unrepen-
tant, unashamed of the one time, the million times when a
rope had been knotted around their neck, when the course of
a man's life had plummeted. They were no better or worse
than we were. They changed species, were transformed into
carnivores when given bodies to eat.

Jeri sat down on the bed and lifted a timid hand toward
Alex's face. She wanted to find her place again. Wanted him
to whisper *I'm afraid* to her, wanted to reassure him that there

was nothing there anymore, no more crowd, that the trees outside were vegetarian. Wanted him to stammer I'm hot so she could run fetch him some water. Ask for a song, so she could sing *Greens for cash, corn for gold, peas for coins. Greens for cash, corn for gold, peas for coins.* Say that she'd left corn sleeping under his mattress for a month before realizing that all she'd get out of it was a boatload of ants, mice, and cockroaches. Corn for gold? Her naivety amused her now, but at the time, given how her family had sweated over it, she had been shocked by the fact that hope did not go to everyone, that even miracles were restricted goods. She knew that there were homes where people cultivated gold. They planted some in the morning, and by evening it was sprouting like Spanish moss.

Her grandmother Phaedra had given her milk, her time, and her health in such a residence. She'd been paid pittance, and three times a year, received cotton pants cut off at the knees, shoes that were shapeless or too small, skirts with tired elastic, teddy bears missing an eye, suitcases missing their clasps, dead, broken, or dirty objects, but given with great tralala, and cunningly wrapped in a sheet of threadbare fabric which the old woman hauled several miles on her back, then laid at her daughter's feet with a vague sense of guilt.

War broke out when she unloaded her treasure. The bundle met its death in the trash heap. The mother and the daughter, the beggar and the proud, each stalked off to sulk in her respective corner, which was the same one, since the house was tiny. Holding a grudge is an illness of the rich.

Phaedra had salvaged a piece of jewelry, a battered cameo brooch which she pinned to her jacket, only she knew just how, on high mass days. She didn't wear it to impress, but to show up looking proper for the Lord. She felt better coming into church with it, kneeling before the cross with it. Imagining her soul like the straw mat in a spotless kitchen.

It was Easter, the White church had burned down. Remarkably, Blacks and Whites were celebrating the resurrection of the same Jesus under the same roof. That might seem strange, and it was. It bothered Phaedra to find herself seated near her boss, squeezed together, elbows, feet, and Bibles, for once just like her. To avoid unsettling her, she trained her eyes elsewhere and released her amens a moment later.

Jeri remembered beggar Phaedra's embarrassment when the priest called on her to close mass with a song. When she stood up, she dropped her Bible. Her body wavered, then she trotted up to the altar and waited permission to intone *Were you there when they crucified my Lord?* Her hands clasped behind her back, her eyes on the eyes of God.

Never had a White person heard Phaedra's voice, maybe no Black person either, and after so many nasal *thank-yous*, *excuse-mes*, *do-you-need-me-for-anything-elses*, Phaedra's voice might have shriveled up in her throat. But no, her voice was gold, more ardent than the yellow corn in the song. As it took off, it rose, filling the vault of the church, those praying, now those crying, those who were the last, those too broke to have shoes, even a bit of shoe to house their calloused feet, even once a month, were now, as promised, first.

Turning her head to get a better look, Jeri surprised the bos-lady's stupefaction, her compulsion to cover her ears with her lace-covered hands, as if she sensed other words beyond the song, as if desperately seeking a silence suddenly forbidden, permanently lost.

Through the central stained-glass window in the house of the All-Powerful, the sun surged like noon, burning her face and neck which were now just a network of wrinkles and ailing valves. No longer could the boss-lady make out the series of sounds, only the irregular beat of her thwarted blood, the end of a world. How dare she, this hired help? Only a bird sang like that.

The next day, Phaedra had come home from work by the same route, and as always, on foot. What didn't seem right was her pace, little steps by a little person carrying a great burden, not only her domesticity, not only her age, but also shame and sorrow. In the house where gold grew like dandelions, she had been accused of stealing the brooch. Phaedra was mortified, mortified over a worthless brooch.

How do you tell people that story?

How do you talk about the time when you hid all the children in a flour bin to save them from the vicious mastiffs of the Klan? The threat returned each day. They were going to demolish houses, they were going to foul the women's and girls' vaginas, they were going to break the babies' bones, a horde would come while everyone in the shack was slumbering, and wham wham wham wham wham wham wham wham wham wham wham wham wham wham wham

wham wham wham wham wham wham wham wham wham wham wham wham wham wham!

Alex pushed away his mother's hand. "Okay, okay, okay," he retorted, furrowing his wide, stubborn, spoiled, not-easy boy's forehead. He was struggling to be courteous, but in his world, now safe again, sons were men.

Jeri walked out, Zaac followed her, and I remained in the room with the teenager.

"I might need you on Tuesday," he said after a long silence, pulling his computer out from under the blanket. It was decked out with stickers and equipped with tiny speakers. A week from Tuesday at 7:00, Christian Scott, the trumpeter, was going to be playing at the Red Dragon. Tickets were thirty bucks, and the concert would be starting late. Alex knew that Jeri wouldn't let him borrow the car.

The Red Dragon was the only club in town worth mentioning. Nobody went there to drink or talk. What mattered there was the sound, listening to live music, and when it ended, applauding the musicians up on the 4'x 6' stage. I'd been there one evening with Jeri when she'd gotten all dolled up and wanted it to serve some purpose. She wore a suit fitted at the hips and thighs. It wouldn't have made any difference if she'd worn sweatpants. The club was so dark inside, you stepped on people's feet and had to light your way with your phone.

Scott wasn't equal to Miles Davis, but Alex was. As the father of no one and made a bastard by the man who'd taken my name back, I pocketed Alex's childish joy like a gift. "Mom said you don't know how to fish. It's easy, I'm going to show you how. Tuesday afternoon, I'm taking you to the lake and then, in the evening, you're taking me to see Scott." He looked at me, his face resolute. We shook on it to seal the deal. After that, he slept like a rock, hugging his laptop like a teddy bear.

I didn't dare move. This was new, no doubt fragile. I thought of the seedlings under which umbilical cords were buried. According to custom.

When I came out, they cut my cord with a blade dipped in boiling water. They rummaged around inside my mother's belly to pull out the placenta and buried the whole thing in the bush, near the house. Because the job had been long, the midwife demanded more money. My father created a scene. He had started to drink and already had debts. I was his first, I became the oldest son.

When I came out of my mother feet first and without crying, my mother predicted that I would be hardheaded. Others thought of misfortune.

I don't know who covered my placenta and my cord with earth. I don't know why the tree that was supposed to grow up with me somehow caught thorns during the rains and turned into a kapok tree. Later, my mother showed it to me. It marked the start of the path that led to our house, but then we moved, the town changed and a part of the bush surrounding our neighborhood was razed. There were plans to build a hospital, but the entrepreneur in charge of construction left the country with a full belly.

After being chased away by my father and humiliated by thieves, I had gone back to the old house. The kapok tree was still there, so I started digging. I was eaten by worms and gnats and dogs. Banned from the towns, they ruled at the edges and threatened outsiders. There were six, eight, a dozen of them surrounding me, a chorus fighting for their belly and some shelter. The bush was their lair. They'd been there before me, had devoured my entrails.

My eyes came back to Jeri's son, his body wrapped in a plaid quilt sewn by hand by his great-grandmother Phaedra. "There!" I thought, tiptoeing out of the protected room. Despite the rains and adversity, Alex's tree would continue to grow, and just as tenacious as the oak that had appeared in his dream. Alex would always be from here, whether or not others made him feel welcome, whether or not the *Welcome home,* sometimes said like a motto, left a bitter taste in his mouth. Clearly, manifestly, he was American. America was his lot, his only patch of ground. He would never have to dirty his fingernails to find his land.

Going down the hallway to the living room, where Zaac had taken up his job as animal hunter again, I thought of the Scott jazz concert and was angry with myself for promising to take Alex. I knew I couldn't. Next Tuesday at that time, I'd be on a Boeing, reflecting on my two months in Louisiana. Could I call my stay a "vacation"?

True, I hadn't moved like a whirling dervish, and I'd gotten stuck in Baton Rouge, but I hadn't just lazed about either. Zaac and I had hung out here and there gathering clues. That is, Zaac or Jeri, depending on whether Zaac, whose drinking now matched his desperation, could more or less hold himself erect on his legs. "You've done your best, my friend." I held this phrase close, like a child hugs his blanket, and listed the few bits and pieces still left to clear up, the people to see, like Lewis, the archivist at Evergreen.

***

As soon as it was dry and sunny, that is, two days after Alex's nightmare, I went back to the plantation to return the box to the employee who'd lent it to me. Jeri had insisted on driving me there. After a downpour like that, the rains sometimes wiped out the roads or felled trees across them. Better to go with someone who knew the area. Tourists sometimes got lost, or worse.

So Jeri woke me up at dawn, and we set out in the Mustang, equipped with boots, hats, and Zaac's *cut-cut*.

An hour later, we were at Evergreen. We sat on a shaded terrace, rocking slowly on a swing, and waiting for Lewis. Sweat prickled between my thighs. There was something reassuring in this liquid flowing from my pores, melting and taking form again. I was sure of at least two things: I was alive, and it was hot. One last time, I opened the box containing the letters. Everything was there, organized as before.

A few yards from the swing, the archivist was taking care of business with a worker who wore cheap glasses and floppy jeans that tumbled down over his sneakers. The sun was back out again, pounding on their heads, but neither tried to fight it. Like fish in a lake.

A truck arrived, forcing them to move. The driver cut the motor and started unloading maybe fifteen kegs. He worked without slowing, one eye on his watch, probably paid by the hour. Another truck drove up, same scene, but the worker unloading the merchandise wasn't used to the task. Casks slipped out of his hands, he set them upright, cursing and spitting on the ground as if reproaching the soil for causing him so much trouble with these products which the earth had promised to every human being. "Puta Madre!" We exchanged looks as he slammed the tailgate shut, and I ducked my head to blow my nose.

The air stank of rot and sugar because of the cane. They cut the stalks into pieces, then ground them into juice that they left to macerate and simmer forever. Jeri explained it to me generally, but she didn't know much about it. Her information came from Auntie Joe's husband who had been an agricultural laborer.

Above the barn from which the odor was emanating, I noticed a cloud of dark haze. It was my turn to spit, not convinced that this vapor was good for the lungs. Those who toiled away there and inhaled it 24/24 would have grounds to complain. After all, we were in this harsh, bitter South. Where the soil had made human beings, the soil continued to take human beings, where humans and the soil were wed for better or worse, where the song of the soil had become a hymn. The individual was not conceded.

Lewis handed a document to the employee who now seemed annoyed with the sun, and hitched up his pants and shoved his glasses up on his nose. There was nothing to read there, no space for his opinion, just sign his name at the bottom and get back to work. Lewis tossed him another comment, then in no hurry strolled in our direction, hands on her hips, her midsection stubbornly round.

Now, watching her outside her office, I suspected that her kin were all rednecks. I sensed in her stride the mindset and awkwardness of the planter. I'd have bet my hand that some of her ancestors had owned slaves. I'd have bet my arm that, alongside her archival skills, she knew the market rates for cotton and sugar plus the time needed to let fields lie fallow between harvests, and that she could detect indolence or sturdiness in a person, and she made sure that the plantation continued to operate, just like Heiner, the guide. I had caught sight of him on the main path. He was coming from the master's house clutching some papers and his thermos.

Lewis went into her office, then came back toward us, carrying a rocking chair, which she slid onto. Her feet didn't touch the ground, her round brown eyes studied us, especially Jeri, with a disconcerting familiarity.

She called to Heiner with a high whistle and a slight wave. "He's a good man, Edgar. He comes from Charlotte. His only fault is his wife. Hey, Heiner! Get back in here, we need coffee! I understand not wanting to eat pork fat. But Heiner's wife goes too far. She has a complex about her cheeks being chubby, so, she's fallen into a never-ending series of diets. She's been demolishing herself for five years to make herself skinny as a nail. What's most pitiful is that she's succeeded, she's lost weight everywhere, but not in her cheeks. So now she won't leave the house. She says: when I pat my cheeks, it feels like touching buttocks."

Lewis settled all her weight on her seat and used the momentum to rock back and forth several times. "Poor Edgar!" It wasn't a groan, just a simple remark. Her hair was too white to feel sorry. But what grieved her was having lost so many things in so little time. Last week's rains had swallowed her house and the Lexus that she had just bought. "Oh shit, oh shit" intoned Heiner who had now joined us on the terrace.

I said that I was heading back to France in a few days. "You don't live in Africa?"

It was Heiner who asked.

"Do you know how many Americas you can fit into Africa?" Jeri retorted drily, crossing her legs. Maybe she had noticed the archivist's persistent stare on her. A sunny and good-natured look, but the struggle for peace has no morals. "Three of them," continued Jeri in the same tone. "Africa is a continent. You come from Charlotte, and he comes from a city which is located in a country."

Jeri went quiet, we were all quiet. And the South resumed its rhythm: the chains of the porch swing squeaking, the wooden floor creaking, the birds jazzing, the squirrels skittering about, the wind rustling, the water rippling, the men working, and further in the distance, the highway.

There are those who leave and those who stay. I wanted to stay on this bench, sit still and sweat, know that there were seasons, foresee a community's eternity with the same aplomb as Mary in Tremé. *Nola will always be Nola.* She could swear to it because her people had been dying there for two hundred years. I wanted to hear the leaves sing when they fell in February, I wanted the moss, the corn on the stalks, I wanted to be able to worry about nothing, just light the lamps because night was falling.

We stood up to leave. I returned the box to Lewis who shook my hand. Heiner wished me good luck, I answered the same, imagining all the tourists who would thrill to his stories, and his wife. I imagined her literally as a nail.

In the parking lot, I blew my nose and spit again. The odor was stuck in my throat. What a stench, that cane! No kidding, it was like sticking your head in a garbage can. I hadn't smelled anything the day I'd come with Zaac. Maybe because it was raining that day, maybe because cane sweats in the sun.

Before driving through the iron gate of the plantation to get back to the highway, Jeri took a left onto a dirt road that ran along a cane field. She had sunk back into her sorrow, was driving a little too fast for this rutted path, moving at the same speed as her thoughts. But the Mustang held out.

With crazed laughter, she parried the undisciplined bits of gravel smacking into the windshield, conquered the mud, dodged the branches and bagasse that the wind and rain had dragged out of the cane fields. I clutched the armrest, my mind crowded with images. I recalled a scene from *The Misfits* with

Clark Gable, when a wild horse galloped around like this. It took a truck, a tire, lassoes, and three cowboys to exhaust the animal's fierce energy. I also thought of the jailbirds at Angola, who at this time, or *asteur* as some say here, were training to be rodeo heroes.

A curious phenomenon, these rodeos where the prisoners played Clark Gable. The Angola prison organized one every Sunday in October. The spectators were crazy about them, and so were the fake cowboys. Mounted on bulls or broncos, they risked their convict skins for hurrahs that gave them the illusion of being redeemed, whatever the offenses they'd committed.

In the arena at Angola, there were no dealers, thieves, rapists, incestuous fathers, good-for-nothings, small-time criminals, big-time criminals, sadists, bank robbers, pimps, perverts, psychopaths, serial killers, or murderers in the first or second degree. There was no hate or fear among the men. The men joined forces against the animals. The animals were the bad guys incarnate.

After a half-hour of bucking along, Jeri stopped the vehicle and we got out. It started after the field, between the stalks yet to be cut and crushed and the bayou still swollen with water. It was a small collection of cabins built close together, with a few cars, and laundry hanging on the lines. It was more than that: slave quarters like the ones that had existed in the past, but the Blacks who had been packed in there were now Mexicans.

Under a pavilion which had never been repainted, a group of men were drinking beer and listening to music. I recognized the employee who had talked to Lewis earlier. His shirt was off, he was red and scarred underneath. A work accident, probably. He leaned down to rummage through a cooler, then asked someone sitting just inside a hovel if there was any Coke left. The flesh figure, who was painting her toenails, reminded him that she wasn't his maid and that the store was closing soon. The man hesitated, then sat back down.

He didn't seem discouraged. He also didn't seem to realize that history was repeating itself. Men were taken on to reduce them to pieces, they were flattened, ground down, and their blood grilled to medium rare, cooked in their very veins, thickened to a toxic syrup.

I turned toward Jeri. She had gone back to the car. "You know," she confessed, after she'd managed to get the car started, "my mother waited until the age of fifty to put my father out of the house. Not because she had her eye on another man, but because his smells, his needs, and his ways had become intolerable. She waited until she'd stopped having a period and was past the legal age for wearing a miniskirt before ending her marriage and enduring her solitude. She did it the instant she could."

Jeri's voice was teary, but her fearless gaze remained steady on the road. She accelerated, zigzagging to avoid loose stones and the remains of cane before the sky could change its mind or the Mustang could rebel. For the moment, only a light drizzle was falling, a fine, tickling rain that the wind hurled into the cane fields. And those two worlds, mineral and vegetal, had a good laugh together. So much so that Jeri, who had opened the windows a crack to clear up the fog on the windshield, had to roll them back up all the way. She said, "We can't hear each other," when she was the only one chattering, going right into other events in her mother's life, an existence neither remarkable nor small, but women, especially when they grow older, are obsessed by their mother.

"Always thinking we're not ready, it's always been that way, been our misfortune. For example, when they told us that slavery was over, many of us rushed into the big house. It wasn't freedom they dreamed of. What they wanted first was to have the master's belongings."

I just reached up for the grab handle and closed my eyes, let my body rock. If I'd been a free man, I would have jumped out of the moving vehicle just for fun, just for the pleasure of getting soaked, just so I wouldn't give a shit about the old masters or the new cabins with Mexicans.

* * *

The Mustang squealed as we pulled out onto the county road. The paved surface flew up at the windshield like a body. The road, with the lying signs promising rest stops, the splashes of houses and star-spangled banners, the heavy sky barely wrung dry, and the fields of some kind of yellow or white grain. That same old route that let us pause for a moment at the Supreme

Catfish Diner #2—I had met Jeri at #1—where Zaac was waiting for us at the bar.

Zaac was coming from the mall where he'd run into a girl who looked like Amber. Not the damnable, loathsome Amber of three months ago, but the one who had her own nice way of sitting when she wore a skirt, of twisting her earrings when she was being coquettish—love, really, it doesn't take much. Yes, that's exactly the Amber he had tailed in the shopping mall where they sold so much junk. And they say people don't have money . . .

Zaac touched his neck, it still stung. There was not a single place where he had not gone to gaze at the Amber-copy.

The waitress at the Supreme Diner, who had no patience for hollow dreams and had heard enough of these inanities, snatched the menus out of our hands and decided for us: French fries, chicken wings, and fried fish with cocktail sauce, because they were out of cheese sauce.

She had to repeat the order because her colleague in the kitchen was hard of hearing, then she found us a table for three right next to the toilets and a fan that was rattling like a refrigerator on the edge of collapse. Jeri shot a look at the fan, the only one of the three vaguely functioning. She wanted to sit elsewhere, but elsewhere was taken and Zaac was too limp to move from this table.

Forearms planted on the plastic tablecloth, Zaac persisted in taking us back to the shopping mall where, after a morning of trailing Amber who wasn't Amber, he had approached her. That was a mistake. The girl snubbed him and he who, deep down was a sweetheart, felt like he had to spit in her face. He kissed his open fists noisily. "After all, I have my honor. I'm a quality guy."

None of us spoke after that. With surly silence we greeted the stale rolls, breaded chicken, beers, fries, ketchup, and six-and-a half cold catfish fillets. It all arrived separately, in random order, and with frowns. The waitress was looking for a fight and was about to find one.

A pile of bones with crooked teeth, Zaac heaped insults on the waitress. He hurled vulgarities at her when she came out of the kitchen, and aimed little bread spitballs at her. He aimed at her feet and would not let up on his bombardment until he'd finally grown bored with this idiotic game.

Key to a squabble is its absurdity. It comes from nowhere and goes nowhere. We had already settled the bill and were waiting for our change at the bar when Jeri made some remark to Zaac that stuck in his craw. Or maybe it was the other way around: Zaac was bad-mouthing the waitress, Louisiana, America in general, he was running down the list of what he called *Crimes against Black Humanity in America*, when Jeri abruptly retorted, "Then get the train moving, if you're a man."

Like that day in her Mustang when she'd scolded her son over a tiny quarrel and dumped him out on the sidewalk like a sack of rice, Jeri had irritated Zaac, who told her to go to hell. He grew angry, she grew angry, they grew angry. She sneered, he sneered, they sneered. He shouted, she shouted,

they shouted. Their voices overlapped and they repeated themselves like hip-hop samples until a man who was a man, the
boss at the Supreme Diner, made them shut their big mouth.

To picture the scene, you have to know what an American
diner is like on Sunday in a neighborhood where most of the
businesses and churches close at noon. You need to imagine
the dapper customers and their bearing when they enter, the
relaxed face with a reserved smile in the middle. You will have
no idea what's going on at their home.

On Sunday, the diner isn't a pawnshop or psychiatric
hospital, or employment agency, or courtroom. It's a chill place
where you come to eat at a reasonable price, drink to be happy,
and engage in light conversation.

After shutting us in the unisex restroom to remind us of
the purpose of a diner, *his* diner, the owner told us how he
viewed life. He was not going to let this business which he
had built from the ground up thirty-five years ago fall into
chaos. He was also not going to let us ruin his Sunday after
he'd slaved away all week. The weekend was for him, he only
came to check on his *empire* in an emergency. And now that
he was on the premises, standing before "three jokers who
were pissing everyone off with their problems," he didn't see
any emergency. He was sorry to have interrupted his day,
wasted his time, his wheels, and his gas for nothing. For
nobody.

Though he appeared calm, it seemed like he could lose
his temper pretty quickly. We gauged his fists and immediately

knew where we stood. We understood that, moral questions aside, punching had never been a problem for him.

Jeri looked at me, I looked at Zaac, Zaac looked at Jeri. We all agreed: it was time to apologize and clear out.

* * *

When the thought was convenient, Jeri imagined the hearts of human beings as little whirring electrical machines that only needed to be rewound to beat in the other direction. She told herself that happiness was a decision, and she was counting on me to inoculate her from Zaac. In the diner parking lot, after she and Zaac had patched things up and had a good long hot sob together, Jeri insisted on going home alone. With Jeri at the wheel, the Mustang drove off in a cancan of convulsions and black smoke. She left us men on our own.

Indeed, there was nothing like a man to idiotically declare war on a mosquito an eighth of an inch long, swearing that he'd smash him with his beat-up shoe or his hand while driving. Just to annoy him. It wasn't the mosquito's exasperating racket, but its nerve. Teensy and invisible, the mosquito continued its impudent pirouette above our heads. Ever since we'd cleared out of the Supreme Diner and set off on the road to Plaquemine, it had been the big shot, the king of the pick-up.

We were going to visit Uncle Cristal, Zaac's godfather. A friendly visit. Just to say hi and talk for a while. In America,

Cristal is not usually a man's name. But that was a long story, so Zaac would explain some other time.

From under his seat, Zaac pulled the remains of an adult magazine, which he rolled up into a weapon and handed to me. "Watch out, they're depraved. They go where they're sure you won't see 'em." The enemy was indeed perverse. I thought I'd obliterated it, but no. As soon as I smashed it, it came back from the dead to bite us behind the ears, nip us on the neck, suck blood from our fists and our shins. "Goddammit!" Zaac brayed, scratching his calves and his forearms until they bled. "Shit! Kill it!" Bzzz . . . Smack! Missed. Bzzz . . . Smack! Missed. This defeat, though small—tiny—threw me into a state of disarray totally out of proportion to the situation. It had me muttering on the weakness of my heart.

Would I have been more stout-hearted if I'd been born in one of those project houses laid out like clusters of nits on the outskirts, and emphatically not in the center of the city? If a girl had betrayed me like the bitch who leaves with the first guy who comes along because he has money and a car and that makes all the difference? If, instead of keeping my pulse, my blood pressure, my standard of living, and my afro from getting too high or too low, I'd taken real risks like a cowboy, if I'd had to, as a father, if I'd found the guts to drag myself down to the police station to identify my son's body, as if death were an exact science? That night when the telephone rang to announce the worst that can happen to a parent, my guess is that I wouldn't have had the strength to pick up.

Zaac grabbed the magazine from my hand, and with a roar, smacked the dashboard to flatten the insect. The pick-up swerved, but Zaac didn't care. Pinched between his fingertips, he was dangling the remains of the mosquito whose location he'd picked out by ear. He patted his thighs with pride. He flipped down his visor to stick his trophy there, and it was not the first. Scattered all over the mirror were scraps of butterfly wings, spider legs, gnats, boogers. He put his hands back on the wheel, pressed the accelerator, and in a few minutes we were at Cristal's house.

Unless you liked canal locks, there was nothing to see in Plaquemine. Nothing special at Uncle Cristal's house either, besides a birdcage, a table that took up space, "The first thing you put in a house is the kitchen table," two clocks set to different times, and a sideboard filled with plates and framed portraits, including one of a soldier and another of a young woman dressed in violet and yellow. She was the youngest daughter of Zaac's godfather and worked in the hospital at Tulane.

Cristal brought out a bottle to drink to her health. He squinted and explained, through his pipe-smoker lips, "She's a surgeon." Then he inhaled a gulletful of his homemade hooch whose recipe he refused to give out because it had taken years of perfecting and he hoped to turn it into a business someday. He burst into laughter. He was glamorizing. It was just fermented cane, citrus, and satsuma.

He filled the three stemmed glasses, and this time we toasted his son Curtis who had gone off to "fuck" the war in Mali, instead of being content with the piece of land that Cristal had turned over to him so he could raise chickens, grow trees for shade, build a little shed for the barbecue, everything you need. But young people . . .

He let go of that sentence to take up others until his wife Gloria walked in. Everyone called her The Queen because she had sung with big names, and nothing scared her. *I don't care who I meet, even if I meet Satan* . . . The parakeet in its cage and Cristal in his armchair repeated it after Gloria who, in addition, was a good cook. In her kitchen, which everybody had to stay out of, she was making shrimp and rice.

I felt heavy as lead when I got back into the pick-up. If you'd heaved me into the bayou, I would have stayed there.

As we drove out of Plaquemine, Zaac was making big plans. He would talk to Curtis, not for Curtis but for the uncle, and would remind him that land is golden. He asked what I thought. Did I, African French that I was, have a piece of land that I could attach myself to, when I grew old? I stared at the asphalt, the sky, and the sun, which any minute now would infuse everything with an amaranth glow. "I guess so." The words came out by themselves, maybe because the feeling came by itself, naturally, the moment you were prepared to take up a rifle or give your blood to keep your land. The words, coming so naturally, were accompanied by the image of a table and chairs, set with plates, a table made of a solid wood, like cypress.

I asked Zaac what his house was like, the one he'd had before knowing Amber. He looked surprised. He had never lived alone. His women had been his houses, and before them, his mother. "What Cristal says is true," he added, clearing his throat to belch, "The table is important when you move in somewhere." The bed counted too, but you couldn't arrange the bedroom just any which-way. In his grandmother's day, you didn't sleep with your feet pointing toward the door. If your feet looked at the door, death would tug on them and your whole body would come to attention, ready to follow.

He shrugged. Those were superstitions. Before, people mostly just slept where it was permitted.

The wolf ate the dog. Day veered into night. Zaac accelerated and I stuck my head out the window to watch the pages from the magazine fly away.

* * *

Like two brothers, two buddies decked out for a party, we sped toward the Big Easy, hooked up with women for a laugh, acted crazy, also did battle, spitting in the face of the last confederates. It was only a matter of months. With the blessing of the ancestors and the solemnity of soldiers, the statues would soon be in smithereens and we would organize a century of drunken revelry.

"Down with the Southerners!" yelled Zaac, at the foot of Jefferson Davis who, even in bronze, even done for, remained obdurate, extending his arm and standing ramrod straight on his pedestal.

Walking down Rampart Street, I caught sight of Mary, sitting on her stoop. She was joking with Paul and Mrs. Crouch, but we were moving too fast to hear. I told Zaac to honk anyway, it was my way of saying See you! You don't say goodbye to old people.

Before getting back on Route I-10 to Baton Rouge, we made a stop at Whole Foods on Magazine Street. The supermarket for the monied was closed, but we could still get into the covered parking lot behind the building. We parked near the emergency exit. I kept watch, in case the security guard came along, while Zaac took a piss over by the trash cans, his fly the whole way down. He was bellowing, "I piss on you all!" as he tried to soak the handles of the shopping carts. He was imagining the first customers' revulsion when they got out of their scented automobile and inhaled the stench. "Down with Whole Foods! Down with Amber and Miss America!" I had to gag Zaac to avoid a mishap. I had promised to keep an eye on him.

Day was dawning when we pulled up in front of Jeri's house. Zaac dragged himself as far as the sofa. I retreated to the bathroom where I shaved and rinsed off with the energy of an EMT reviving an accident victim. Earlier, on the road coming back to Baton Rouge, I had decided to push back the date on my return ticket. I could not see myself embarking on a trip in just two days, and pulling my bag off the conveyer belt, shouting, "Bonjour Paris, Merci, Jeanne!" Jeanne had offered to come to pick me up at Roissy. "I've put all your belongings in a box. We have to figure out what we're doing." She'd warned me.

I contacted the airline and requested ten days' grace. Enough time to say goodbye to Louisiana, which, with all its muck, had me in its bed. Louisiana had softened me up as only a skilled whore can.

In the kitchen where I made toast and savored my first coffee of the day, Jeri was busy concocting her anti-cat poison. Aiming to liquidate the seven felines next door, she had poured five hundred milligrams of acetaminophen into a mortar and was pulverizing it with the pestle, her lips bitter and tight. "The last time," she was talking about the keen-sighted beasts, "they paid no attention to the mixture that I'd prepared for them. They eyed me as if seeing into my heart." I didn't know enough about the psychology of cats to have an opinion. What I could confirm, on the other hand, was that one cat could hide another and consequently, it was always better to be careful. Jeri looked up from her pulverized concoction to think. She needed more than a proverb. So, I told her about the miseries of a man as poor as a pebble, who had captured a full-sized Persian cat to stave off dying of starvation and had boiled him without skinning him. It was furry, so he'd hoped that meant it would be meaty. What a shock, what a calamity to discover that once cooked, the Persian cat was as small as a mouse.

I wasn't going to guarantee the authenticity of the tale, but I was happy to see that it pleased Jeri whose gaze, now turned to the garden as if seeing it for the first time, was once again soft and bright like the moon. Outside the window, the wind made the flowers and the leaves on the tree branches nod. It jostled the youngest lemons. It exasperated the most mature fronds on the palm tree, and they floated down to the lawn in a gentle cascade, a sigh of capitulation. The laws of nature. There was no man behind all that.

Jeri lit a cigarette for the pleasure of taking a puff. Her back to me and still attentive to the swaying of the wind, she asked me if the story of my uncle departing from Cameroon on an adventure and then dying here was true. It wasn't a question. She was admitting that she'd never believed it. She hadn't wanted to meddle or embarrass me. But since I leaving soon, she wanted to reassure me, let me know that I no longer needed an excuse to stay or to come back to Louisiana.

Engulfed by a wave of fatigue, I set my cup of coffee down on the table. I felt my body go numb, then contract. I felt it become one with the wooden bench under my buttocks, the four feet of the table, the tight floorboards, the beams across the ceiling. My body was like a house of cypress. I was present like I had never been before.

Jeri tossed her half-smoked cigarette in the kitchen sink. She was right: I had treated the facts as a convenience. Conveniently, I had retained only one part of my great uncle's biography. In the longer version, the one my mother had taken pleasure in unpacking for me on the eve of my departure, over my protestations, the bushman had not ended his life in Louisiana, he'd ended his days in Douala, in a bar where even my father, *the other*, never would have dared to set foot. My mother never talked about the poorly lit *buvettes* where men and women sat with their backs to the street and the poverty, where talking meant shouting because of the music. The more the music cranked up, the more beer that went down, inevitably. She described the private clubs where deflowered girls rubbed their crotch up and down on poles and lap-danced customers. They could only be hunted down with money, tucking one or two thousand-FCFA bills between their breasts or into a G-string which who knew where it had been. Once back from Louisiana, Etienne John Wayne Marie-Pierre had a fling with one of those shrewd girls. And even if the affair meant everything and nothing in Douala, my mother was sure that the little idyll had gone bad, both for the woman who had never been seen again at the club and for the uncle who had turned into a *crevard*, a freeloader.

In the country, *crevards* are less-than-dogs. They go around, hands dangling at the sides of their dangling bodies. You see them in front of service stations, you honk to avoid running them over, but after a while you pay them no attention. In the country, *crevards* are former human beings. They used to have trade and a roof over their head, but the magic ruined them. They always blame the magic.

"Everyone dies the best way possible, but there's no such thing as a beautiful death," Jeri concluded after hearing this version of the story. Etienne John Wayne Marie-Pierre had done life. End of story.

From the parking lot, we took a path that led us a few yards to the contained banks of the lake. Clans of ducks and geese were swooping about. A white heron was doing acrobatics. A few green oaks offered shade to the fisherman who had come to pull perch and crappies from the fresh water with all the gear of early-rise experts.

Alex would have arrived before them if he had listened to himself, but with Zaac underfoot, time trickled away. There were always a couple of things that had to be done between two important things to take care of. As a result, nothing happened the way it should. They always got something going at the last moment, which was always the moment it was too late.

Alex made his arguments, but Zaac refuted them: "There's no best time to catch fish." That said, as we were getting settled, Zaac eyed every bucket, every fishing pole, every fish pulled from the water with longing, and sighed when he saw a fisherman moving to a new place or shifting his strategy. "Of course, you'll end up getting a bite if you move around all the time. But fishing should be elegant." (He was only addressing me because Alex was pouting.) "It's an art. If a fish comes, it comes. If it doesn't come, it doesn't come. Sometimes you think a lake is sleeping and suddenly, some guy right next to you lands ten in a row. It's both art and fate."

Alex slipped his iPad into its case, took his fishing rod, and moved farther away. His four-foot legs sent the quacking ducks scattering. He was enjoying this. Really seemed comfortable in his shoes.

They all seemed comfortable in this environment, the men waiting for a nibble on the line, the women and children around them. A little girl wearing a pink life jacket was helping her father, handing him maggots. A couple sitting near an ice cream stand was flirting. Women in festive warm-up suits were reveling in beignets and fried chicken. They were letting the time roll, the good times at a good price, it cost nothing to be here.

I looked up at Zaac and saw him turn his head toward the clouds as if hoping for a sign before he got started. He had donned his wide-brimmed bucket hat, pulled it down so far that you could only see the bottom half of his face, misshapen by the wad of gum he was chewing. He stopped ruminating, started again, stopped again, then planted his line in the water, spreading his legs a little and studying the bottom of the lake. He was saving himself for the most beautiful fish and had equipped himself accordingly. "The longer your line, the bigger the fish you'll catch. Makes sense." But first you had to know how to bait a line, and in my case, that had taken all morning.

Zaac grabbed me by the shoulder and pointed a finger at the opposite bank. He was looking at a little bush that was gliding along the dark, muddy surface. "See that?" All I could see was brambles, grass, and water. "That's the best spot. I bet they're over there. I can feel it. Fishing is a feeling."

Again, I scanned the spot which Zaac estimated to be "three feet deep," and waited for the freshwater fish to emerge. There was nothing else to do for the time being, just keep an eye on any movement and pull one in.

Zaac's total haul was two fish, but with Alex's catch, we had enough for dinner. We would light the charcoal, relax on the terrace, savor the flesh, and suck the bones until the cats were riled.

"Next time!" Alex promised, seeing that my bucket was empty. With strips of fabric and rubber bands, he stowed his equipment and bucket in the bed of the pick-up truck, then jumped in himself, to take in the breeze. As the truck headed back to Jeri's house, he would close his eyes. He would imagine the sea, or the big city. Baton Rouge sucked, for sure. Damn capital with no head, no navel, no center, no place to park, even though nothing ever happened there. In the evening, you watched the hours grind past, all the people grind past, cars, old people, young people, the streets, the river. He would think about the clothes that he was going to wear to the Red Dragon, how he'd lace up his basketball sneakers, set his cap at the right angle, adjust the strap on his shoulder bag, pat on some cologne. At that age, every detail counts.

* * *

Alex insisted on being close to the stage, so we sat right up front. Everyone applauded for a good five minutes as Scott made his way through the room to join the musicians already hanging out on stage. He didn't traverse the hall at once. In the Dragon's filtered light, he advanced slowly, and after each stride, blew on his trumpet do-re-mi's that spread far, all the way to the Mississippi it seemed.

From where we were sitting, we could only make out the outline of the trumpeter and his audience. Good Lord! A crowd before its leader, a crowd who let him pass, who passed him along. Scott was being carried.

The moment he reached the stage, two spots revealed him in dabs of light. The audience could take in the details: the folds-wrinkles of his harem pants, the chubby cheeks, and his gold. He was wearing as much as my father's buddy, a political hack who dreamed of being buried with rings and pendants, chains and a gold centurion belt buckle because he thought gold doesn't go anywhere, no matter what you become: old, ugly, sick, skinny as a nail, like Heiner's wife. That, and owning a jet, was this man's wish.

His shoulders, his whole torso leaning into it, Scott put his trumpet to his lips. "This is for the ancestors," he said. Which included a ton of people, from Blacks sealed up in the holds, lashed, hanged, struck down by bullets, to the last great tribes who, for believing that the earth should be shared, had come out with a ridiculous, unseemly share. Pittance!

I noticed the fine gold snake that circled his upper arm, just a jewel, but it looked alive, each contraction of his muscle shaking its mouth and tail. Scott could definitely feel all the eyes fixed on this ornament, and knew that everyone, like me, was expecting to see the reptile start wriggling for real, and the stage turn into woods, prairie, fields, swamp. He knew the power of his jazz. It was a medicine or a charm, if you will, to calm, to bring happiness and make it endure, so that once we're home again, each of us at home and God with us there, we may all smile as big as bananas, we may all store our problems under glass. Tomorrow is always another day.

Already, Alex was beginning to relax. He had pulled off his cap, stopped picking at his jeans, lost interest in the "W" top of the cute girl who was selling drinks. He kept his eyes on the show, the trumpet, the snake, the musicians who could have been his good friends, their passion, too, and that's why there was so much admiration and envy in his eyes when he whispered, "Check out the bassist!" and "Check out the pianist!" That's why he applauded the solos at any time, tilting his head, like Scott, as he tripped on the musicians' prowess.

As a young man, I'd searched like that, too. After a Prince concert, after seeing him dance, I'd practiced doing the splits in my bedroom. I wasn't too bad at going down, I could do that okay, but coming back up was completely different. Impossible without hands.

I recognized *The Big Chief*, a piece which had played on the radio the day I arrived in Baton Rouge. Scott explained where it all came from, that song, his repertoire in general, his values and his ideas. They had all come down to him from his uncle Donald Harisson, Jr., who had inherited them from his father Donald Harisson, Sr., an authentic Black Indian, a product and herald of the coalition between runaway Blacks and American Indians. The two had joined forces against the White oppressor. That had resulted in a culture, a tradition.

The word wasn't bogus in the trumpeter's mouth, it was alluvium, a manifesto. Dispersed today, we came from somewhere. Tossed about for ages, we had plazas, juke joints, Congo Squares where we could gather.

The drummer lashed his cymbals, as if striking nanny-goat hides. The audience clapped along. The trumpet wailed like a conch shell. I closed my eyes to hang onto the notes. To flutter with them, grow dizzy, dance, rub against them, and without tearing myself away from the club, come upon a procession at the bend in a narrow street, discover masks, beads, embroideries, mirrors, and in the middle of insanely corpulent plumage, maybe pick out a pair of wide-open eyes and the silent mouth of a Black Indian. I have to say, it was impressive.

It could have been midnight or noon, we could have been above or below old New Orleans, we marched behind them, chiefs, queens, spies, inscrutable kinglets but so proud when photographed. We trotted along happy, sweaty, uncultured. Behind the show, dueling songs, the heavy, expensive costumes, the mystery was preserved.

The jazz stopped as abruptly as it had begun. Scott impro-
vised a few white-hot notes, then the whole Red Dragon rose
in applause. We also applauded the musicians who, under the
harsh lights and without their instruments, looked like Alex's
little brothers. Scott called them "the kids" but promised that
we'd hear more about them: they were the backup team. He
stuck his dwarf trumpet under his arm and hitched the snake
up high. The beast had been pacified. All we could see of it
now was one end. The rest had disappeared under the sleeve
of his polo shirt. When Scott came down from the stage, Alex
turned toward him. "Good job, man." That was it, but for Alex,
it was gold, and his fists plunged into his pockets, his rolling
shoulders spoke for him, testifying to his condition of growing
young man. For being a man was a trade. You had to prove
that you had what it takes.

Scott went over to the bar and bought beers for the kids.
Now he was thirsty. No trace of exhaustion or passion showed
on his face. The whole time he was drinking, we didn't budge.
Me, I was still riveted by the scene, and Alex, swaying on his
feet.

* * *

We left the club after the group did. Getting home took
a while because the Mustang kept stalling out and because
none of us wanted to see the night end. I no longer knew
what I would give or give back to Jeri when she opened
her arms and her thighs to me, when the fire, which was not
arousal, shone in her eyes. Last night, after the love, she

had gazed at me the way she looked at her band of saints glued to the ceiling of her car that was ready for the junkyard. She dreamed of a hero or nothing. We'd smiled about it, but the weight of those black ghosts tightened my heart now, as I was approaching her room and the moment when her door would close behind us.

Alex, his eel-like body curled up in a ball in the passenger seat, was staring out at the broken lines dividing the lanes on the highway. As he counted the stripes, his lips moved, the only visible part of his face otherwise hidden behind the lowered hood of his sweatshirt.

We drove just to drive through the scraggly streets of the city. At this hour, only the crazies and the poor were about. We spotted them just at the last second and could believe they were spirits or something else: a crooked pole, a tree shaking in the wind. When I remarked on them to Alex, he paused in his counting to remind me why the city was called Baton Rouge. It was a French invention. In the olden days, while exploring the banks of the Mississippi, a Frenchman had come across an immense cypress with red trunk and needles. The trees had made him think of a stick and the name had stuck.

The cypresses in Jeri's neighborhood that soaked up to their knees in the lake were bluish and teary. They scared me each time I passed them. Like birds of misfortune all lined up, or bewitched butterflies, they always left me sad and worried.

We went back through the city center, drove past city hall, and came to a street that led us to Spanish Town. The neighborhood was no more than a modest bundle of colorful houses. After the last side street came the zone. We came to a collection of misshapen apartment buildings gripped by a menacing silence.

The Mustang screeched when I tried to put it in reverse, so I continued moving forward with the windows rolled up. As soon as I could, I turned toward the light onto an opulently curved avenue with a fringe of lampposts and strips of lawn. Rolling the windows down again, I noticed that Alex was asleep. He had dropped off abruptly, his head thrown back as if unscrewed, not distrustful in this car that could have been taking him anywhere.

In the Peugeot that had carried me far from Yaoundé, I had entrusted myself to my mother with the same docility. After a two-night stay with her godmother, she had stuck us on a plane, a train, then a bus. She'd made me wear socks with my sandals. She kept saying, it's cold here, even though I was dying of heat and embarrassment. Then Mathieu was born, and we lived as three.

It was late but all the lamps at Jeri's house were still on. The TV was on full blast, playing a romantic comedy about an African prince who had come to America to find a wife. In the frosty streets of sky-less New York City, His Majesty Murphy was wandering around with his stack of trunks, his talk, his advisors and a simplicity that those he encountered automatically assumed of him.

"You have to be American to get it," Jeri wisecracked, her square frame on the sofa, and leaned forward, rocked her whole body forward to laugh better.

Alex staggered toward his room. I collapsed on the terrace where right away Boxer the cat leaped onto my lap. He softened up like a stuffed animal when you scratched his muzzle and back end, he begged for love, whining like a child.

At one point, he turned his gaze up toward the roof, and I wondered what he was thinking, if he'd worked out a plan to clear out the rodents. We couldn't hear them yet, but I knew they would start galloping over the shingles as soon as we went to bed. Their commotion was never-ending. You'd have to burn down the city to destroy them.

To prove that he was on my side, Boxer got back up on his paws and bobbed his head. He stopped whining and his eyes gleamed.

I let the day break, the sun come up and the rain come down, mute velvety dew that enveloped me like a protective coating, an extra skin, a fabric over my skin. I filled my lungs to the max and held the air up high in my chest, as high and as long as possible, seventeen seconds before going into the void, five, two, and release. Lay down my share of the bile and pain and stop me at the bone when I feel my ribs. I emptied my lungs and got up to pack my suitcase.

I heard steps in the entrance hall and the sound of. someone making noise in the kitchen. It was Zaac, who had come in from the darkness outside, ravenous as a tiger and craving beignets. Deep in his hollow, piss-yellow eyes, I detected a desire to see me stay. Until the very end, he would purr, make yourself at home, since over there, I didn't have any land, since over there, I had been eaten by the dogs.

He changed his clothes and slathered himself with cream, then said he'd treat me to a final pig-out. It was still early, my plane wouldn't leave until four o'clock.

For that reason, because we had time in our back pocket, an eternity, said Zaac, we found ourselves on the asphalt, just floating. And for that reason, after paying for our take-out beignets, we started the pick-up and thought nothing about speed. "We are pharaohs, we are eternal." Zaac was improvising and drumming his fingers on the dashboard to imitate the band. He didn't care if he sang like a saucepan or swerved past cars, he heard nothing anymore, not even the siren of the car tailing us. Not even the voice that summoned us, with no please or sir, to pull over on the shoulder or we were dead men. They would shoot us down. Two of them threatened us. They were possessed by a rage that came from their entrails and sputtered out through the bullhorn.

The pick-up slowed to a halt. Zaac cut the motor. He glanced at his watch before stepping out of the truck. I didn't move. Rooted to the shotgun seat, I watched Zaac in the side mirror. I watched him walk toward the cops.

He moved easy, unhurried, cool. Usually rowdy, Zaac was walking like he owned the road and the law. A stupefying calm took over his body and gave the scene an unreal turn. It affected the cops, who just stood there, powerless to apprehend the individual, a male of average height, black skin, wearing a suit, approaching them so composed.

An odd suit which had belonged to one of Jeri's ancestors, outdated for sure, and too wide, especially on Zaac's frame. Watching him slip into it that morning, I'd said, "Never put on a dead man's clothes." Zaac had turned up the jacket hem with masking tape and snaked a belt through the loops on the pants. I should have explained: Never put on a dead man's clothes because it was bad luck. But you had to be from over there to believe it, you had to have slept in the bush, know that a boa is more than a boa, that cat whiskers will spoil a man. I had unlearned these superstitions, but in Jeri's house that morning, a day of departure, all the sayings, all the warnings of the other old world had come back to me: never borrow the belongings of the deceased, never eat or drink at someone's house, never leave your sweat, urine, hair, spit, underwear, or chewed-off fingernails behind.

Because I wasn't sure what to do with my hands, I laid my palm flat on my heart. My passport and phone were at Jeri's house. All I had was few bucks in my pocket and I had no idea how to get us out of this. All I had was my pounding heart and my eyes on Zaac who was no longer Zaac, just a suit being viewed from behind that looked like a grampa butt with spaghetti legs, as his too-long pant legs chewed the ground.

Wedged inside the pick-up where I'd been happy, I watched the suit stir. Old threads with haloes in the armpits and traces of cheap detergent that ends up costing you when it doesn't rinse out and leaves stains. Someone had gotten married in that suit fifty years ago, someone had felt elegant in it, made his heels click on the floor as he strutted up to the altar like a showman, and flipping up his jacket collar, had gloried in "my shack, my wife, my suit." And died like everyone else.

Suddenly, it looked like Zaac was lowering his arms to roll up his sleeves. That's what he actually did, then started in again with his, "We are pharaohs, we are eternal, we are pharaohs, we are eternal." Drummed it out. Me, I was whistling the song through my teeth and, of course it was perfect for this stretch of highway where two cops had come to carry out their duty, to enforce the law, which is what they call it when they mean enforce the usual, they're just there to reinforce the usual. Again, they yelled in their bullhorn, ordering Zaac to shove his voice back in his face. One more word, one more move, and they'd shoot.

Zaac, Zaac, lifted his face to the sun, as if to breathe it in, to soak in its grace. He cupped his hands and raised them high, high until his pants looked like pants again. He looked like a champion, his face in the light, his feet dancing.

Like a new groom, an Arab celebrating, a peasant looking over his harvest, like a crowd seeing God, Zaac danced. Not this or that dance, but a nameless dance because it came from all the places where pain and hope lay locked in embrace. In the farthest reaches of the coasts, on the backs of ships, in the quarters, the slave hovels, men and women had danced like this and it had lived on in their bodies, this possibility of resistance.

Zaac danced the blues, the juba, quadrille, gumboot, gwo ka, second line, bullerengue, maloya, funk, maypole, cumbia, palo de mayo, hip-hop, the Ave Maria, for there were prayers in his dance, magic, let's call it the quimbois, juju, voodoo, it came in through the feet, then the sound flowed into his legs, his fingers sang, his hips rolled, it spanned centuries, so many parts of the world, it was so joyful he hiccupped, wet his pants, such strength, such insolence, we had survived, we were there, beautiful, dressed up, standing, proud, dangerous, and we were saying kill-me don't care I am eternal, kill-me don't care I am eternal and fuck you, shit, that's what he was singing, Zaac was, with holes in his pants and the blood dripping from his jacket, that was his song while the two policemen shot him like psychos, sick in the head, sick-in-the-head dogs, White people, even if one of them was of the same color as us, shot him again and again to be sure that this body, trained never to fall, would finally fall, good god, what a struggle, that dance!

How can I go on describing it?

I cleared out of the truck. Quietly, I crawled to the bridge and tipped into the void, into this lake that seemed like an ocean, unpredictable and robust when you dove into it. I swam for a while without looking ahead, I called out to my father for help, not my mother, my father, the powerful one, to come deliver me. The water carried me back to land, and in the mud I slept until I'd been burned by the night.

When I woke up, it was muggy and swarming with mosquitos patrolling like helicopters. A dog howled in the distance. The moon came out and lit up the lake.

Around the island on which I found myself, an island no wider than a canoe, I discovered a ballet of alligators and diagonal cypresses like phantoms emerging from the abyss or from the sky, who knows? Maybe they were coming from above.

My heart stuck in neutral, I raised myself on my elbows, and in my stupor looked around for the bridge. What had gotten into me to jump ship and leave Zaac behind? When he'd parked his pick-up, he'd checked the time. He believed in *I die when I want to*, and it was exactly noon when they shot him like a dog. What they did to him cannot be called killing.

For a second, I inhaled his scent, as if I were holding him, still vigorous, in my arms, and our first outing together came back to me, in this city that's easy, as long as you're seeing it through eyes that are blue, but so hard for us others, the draft-animal men, so mean and callous that after the bars, it was better to sit down and discharge the bitterness, empty your guts on the banks of the river that asked nothing more. It's full of wild beasts down below, you don't see them, but they are waiting for us and devour all that can be eaten. Go ahead and sit there, but not too close, since the beasts are sensitive to noise and the females are crazy.

Zaac had been a promoter for a tour guide who offered trips on the bayou for forty dollars a head. One time he had seen a monster as long as a train. What a scene to escape a thrashing, I remembered the anecdote. He had acted it out so well. That's how you nail a good story.

In the night bleached white by the moon, I thought I saw the lake trembling. A wild animal or cypress, one or the other, was moving toward me. A glimmer. I had to be hallucinating, it happens when you're dying of fright or lack of sleep. I rubbed my eyes. Damn! This was serious, the thing was still gliding along, honest to god, to the howls of the dog, that dog whining at nobody but death, this song to death that filled the lake and my skull. I clamped my hands over my ears to make it stop and leaned back against a decapitated tree whose roots surged out of the earth, like wounded, angular knees. I had never felt so close to calamity. Even during my trip back to the country, I'd taken less of a hammering, going back to see my father so he could rename me, and got nothing but "nada," as if "papa" was too big a word.

I cried over that so I wouldn't cry over Zaac, and I heard Zaac laugh. I caught his laughter as it dove off the bridge and plunged into the lake, dove off the bridge again and plunged into the water, he would die when he wanted, and will never die, that was the secret of Zaachary Ramses II, African American pharaoh.

This laughter that thwarted the curse wasn't coming from just one man. It was also coming from the rebel at the

Evergreen plantation who, after so many mornings, so many years, putting up with that same old song, *Cotton made the South, cotton is the South. Cotton is good for the South and the South is good for cotton. The more labor, the more cotton; the more cotton, the more gold. Cotton is the father and the mother of the Old South*, she had left the big house. It was only afterwards that she'd learned how to steal, barefoot and laughing, I suppose, before holing up in a corner where the dogs and the horses didn't go.

I listened to the arms of the cypress trees cracking, *my arms broke, they broke my arms with rocks* they lost their leaves at the end of autumn *my spine is twisted, they wrenched it* and their naked, twisted carcass scared off the kids.

Then it grew light and hot at the same time. A flock of herons skimmed over the lake's surface. As they sped by, they showed their blue plumage. Also depended on the hour and the light. They turned violet at noon when you were squinting. I took a moment to take in their spectacle and got up to wipe bits of mud off my jeans.

I felt surprisingly calm now, young and strong before this world that the sun, though broad and boiling, had never burned. You could struggle, you could kill, you could die, you could forget, but it was what it was, and would remain that way. It was the Old World, with its savage animals, its martyrs, its ghosts, its eternal living things, and the trees echoing *they ripped out my heart and threw it into the swamp.*

A small world, so small that already I could hear the rumble of a boat, I saw Jeri approaching with her shotgun. I wrapped my arms around her.

they ripped out my heart, they threw it into the brackish swamps and when Master, the morning after, asked them why Thunder them-others had stashed my heart out there, they came back a hundred and a hundred searched the ground then the water, it was early, late, it was always what they were after search, they prattled on about the good Lord, they gave iron to their dogs, but let me tell you, I did not take off, I sat on my knees until they left, until the branches and the moss had grown around me, they ripped out my heart to drown it in the swamps, and when I took it back, and when I raised my body to go back to the country, I no longer had feet, I no longer had arms, I no longer had skin, they tossed my heart into the salty swamp waters, let me laugh: salt preserves the heart, they broke my arms with rocks, they broke my spine with a long rifle, they twisted me, they hanged me, they kill me, they kill me out of habit, but I am eternal, look I am a giant

Acknowledgments

For their assistance, their parler-dire, and their solid support, I thank Madame Joan Rhodes and her clan, the sisters Paulette and Mary, and my neighbors in Tremé, the highly inspired Philippe Aldon, Béatrice Germaine, Consulate General of France and the Alliance Française of New Orleans, friend Philippe Bon, of the Conseil départemental de la Guadeloupe, my dear friends Cécile and Francesca, Mrs. Lynn Franck, Jonathan Mayers, his pick-up and his monsters, Capitaine Masseaut, the talking trees, the spirits of Evergreen and of La Ramée. For their luminous presence, I thank my people, those who have gone before and those who are here still.

Translator's Acknowledgments

I am grateful to many people for their support along the way.

To the Bread Loaf Translators Conference, especially my small group members and our leader Edward Gauvin, whose questions, early on, gave me new ways to think through the text.

To Susquehanna University for our association of over two decades.

To Philip Stelly and Laurie Mayer for their attentive readings and insights into how Louisiana, especially New Orleans, lives and breathes.

To Fabienne for our discussions and to Gladys, who started me on this journey. Two important people in my life.

To my family, this is for you.